I0764877

Set Me Free

Set Me Free

interlude press • new york

ISBN 13: 978-1-941530-80-1 (trade)
ISBN 13: 978-1-941530-81-8 (ebook)
Published by Duet Books, an imprint of Interlude Press
duetbooks.com

Book and Cover Design by CB Messer

10 9 8 7 6 5 4 3 2 1

interlude press • new york

To everyone who believed in me,
this book would not exist without you.

The caged bird
sings of freedom.

—"Caged Bird" by Maya Angelou

Chapter One

"Mama, relax."

Jonas Luckett let himself into the two-bedroom apartment he shared with his mother. He nestled his cell phone between his ear and his shoulder as he spoke. The sun shone through the living room window, and, barely taking time to register the downtown Austin skyline he closed the blinds.

"Jonas, don't you screw this up," his mother's voice boomed. "If you don't get to the bus station on time—"

"Mama, I got it covered," he said. "And you know I hate it when you call me that." A bead of sweat trailed down his cheek, a memento from his fast pace outside. He was thankful that the air conditioner was going full blast. The oppressive summer heat had kicked in early.

"It's the name I gave you at birth, young man," his mother scolded. As usual, though, he could hear the teasing in her voice. "Lucky is not a name for a child."

"I'm not a child, Mama." Lucky grabbed a bottle of water from the fridge and took a large drink.

"Just 'cause you're eighteen doesn't mean you aren't a child," his mother said. He grinned. Dinah Luckett was a spitfire, and she didn't let anyone forget it.

Lucky put the cap on his bottle of water and headed to his bedroom. He'd hoped that his mother would at least be home to see him off, but that was out of the question now. "I wish you were taking me to the bus station," Lucky told her.

"I have to pull a double," Dinah said, repeating what she'd told him at the beginning of her call. "Tracy called in sick, and Becky quit this morning."

"I texted Mr. Roberts. I'm sure he can take me." He paused. "I'm just gonna miss you, that's all."

"I'm gonna miss you, too," Dinah replied. "But this summer's gonna be so good for you. You be sure and thank Mr. Roberts for getting you this job."

Lucky rolled his eyes and sat down on the edge of his bed.

"Of course I'm going to thank him, Mama. I've thanked him like a million times already."

Mr. Roberts had been his favorite teacher in high school. He'd believed in Lucky and supported him his entire high school career. The summer job he'd gotten Lucky was just one more thing he owed the man for.

"Did you pack enough underwear?" Dinah asked. Lucky rested his head in the palm of his hand, glad he was by himself for this particular conversation. Lucky double-checked his bags for the third time. He made sure he had enough outfits to last him between trips to the laundromat. He was planning to go once a week, but he wasn't sure he'd be able to stick to that schedule.

"Yes, Mama."

"I gotta go, Jonas. We just had a crowd of hungry kids come in."

"Okay, Mama. I love you."

"You too." Click and she was gone.

Lucky took a deep breath. This job was the biggest thing that had ever happened to him and he couldn't screw it up. The contacts he could make, the experience he would have, and the paycheck he would earn would all help him when he went to college in the fall.

Lucky scanned his bag of art supplies, ensuring he hadn't forgotten anything vital. He could always try to find an art store later, but it was simpler to bring his own.

Lucky sank down on the bed. He glanced at the various pieces of art that covered the plain white walls of his bedroom. Lucky loved every piece, most of them posters or replicas of famous works. He'd rarely spent a night away from home, let alone a whole summer. He hoped he could sleep without the familiar comforts.

A text from Mr. Roberts distracted him. His former teacher was waiting outside. Lucky hurried to grab his bags. He slung the strap on his duffle bag over his shoulder and held the handle of his portfolio in one hand, his satchel of art supplies in the other. The June heat washed over him and he was sweating by the time he reached Mr. Rogers beat up old pickup.

"That all your stuff?" Mr. Roberts called, getting out of the truck and coming round to the curb to help him load it in the truck bed. Lucky nodded. His bags loaded, Lucky slid into the passenger side of the truck.

Mr. Roberts eased out into traffic. "I think I've lost track of the number of times I've driven you around." After a few moments of silence, he said, "You're not usually so quiet. I thought you'd be bouncing off the walls with excitement."

"I am excited, I just..." he trailed off. Lucky *was* excited. What were the chances someone in his position would get an opportunity like this one? He'd be doing what he loved all summer long, in a beautiful place with all kinds of interesting people. Most kids his age would kill to be in his situation. Still, he was extremely nervous. He would be working at a summer carnival off the coast of Georgia. Though he had worked at local carnivals before, the idea was still intimidating.

"It's a lot, I know," Mr. Roberts said. "But I wouldn't have recommended you for the job if I didn't think you could handle it."

"I know. I just... you've seen what I've done lately."

"Inspiration comes in time, Lucky." Mr. Roberts steered around a corner. "You've got the talent. Everything else will fall into place. Just be patient. You can't rush greatness."

"I hope so," Lucky muttered. "Otherwise there's no point in art school."

Mr. Roberts clapped him on the shoulder. "Believe in yourself. I do."

"Thanks, Mr. Roberts," Lucky murmured. "And thanks for the ride."

"Anytime, Lucky."

Inside the bus station, Lucky paid for his ticket and turned his duffle bag over to the guy loading the baggage and took a deep breath. Facing Mr. Roberts, he smiled what he hoped was a confident smile.

"Have a great summer, Lucky."

"I will." Lucky hugged him and then stepped up into the bus.

This was going to be the best summer ever. Lucky wouldn't let it be anything else.

* * *

"How much longer?"

"Tybee Island isn't *that* far from Savannah, Lyn," Aaron replied. He glanced at Evelyn Rossman, his best friend in the whole world, who was sitting in the passenger's seat. "Are we five again?"

Aaron enjoyed the feel of wind in his auburn hair and the smell of the ocean that his convertible afforded him. Memories of childhood car trips came to mind. When they were kids, they had been too impatient to sit even the short distance to the beach. During those trips he and Lyn had become best friends. They'd spent all their time together swimming, building sand castles, and eating ice cream on the beach. He couldn't imagine a summer vacation without her.

"No." She tapped him on the leg in mock anger and sniffed with false indignation. "Just anxious to hit the beach. A tan this good takes a lot of work, you know."

Aaron glanced at her again. Her long blonde hair was pulled back into a braid for the car ride. Lyn's tan was as spectacular as she'd boasted. She was the epitome of a modern day Southern belle, right down to her peach-colored sundress and expensive sunglasses. Of course, there was more to Lyn than met the eye, but few people were aware of that. Aaron was one of the few.

"Come on, don't act like you haven't been counting down the days," Lyn said.

"Yeah, yeah. Three months with no expectations, what's not to love?"

"The minimal parental supervision doesn't hurt either," Lyn teased.

Aaron chuckled. "She speaks the truth."

"One of these days, Aaron, you're going to figure out that I'm all-knowing and you should always agree with me."

Aaron snorted.

"Hey!" Lyn whacked him on the arm this time. "I'm just saying that you need to lighten up a little this summer."

Aaron frowned at her. "I'm light."

Lyn sighed and looked away. Aaron ignored her mini-pout session and focused on the road. This was not a new conversation for them. In Lyn's eyes, he was too serious, too wrapped up in winning his father's approval to enjoy himself. It was hard to be any other way; his parents had ingrained their expectations when he was young.

"Just promise me you'll talk to your father about Harvard, at least."

Aaron winced. In a weak moment, he'd broken down and confessed that he did not want to go to Harvard Business School as his father had planned. He'd also told Lyn that he had no desire to take over his parents company, Ledbetter, Inc.

"You know I can't," he said.

Silence reigned again, and Aaron resisted the urge to press harder on the gas pedal. His father would flip if he got a speeding ticket.

"Aren't you tired of being perfect all the time?" Lyn asked.

"What?"

"I mean it, Aaron. Isn't it exhausting, always playing the part of the dutiful son? Aren't you just done with doing what our parents expect us to do?"

"No?" Aaron said. "Where is this coming from?" Lyn usually didn't push him like this. Her voice seemed tinged with desperation, but he couldn't imagine why.

"Do you want to marry me?" The question drew a heavy silence into the convertible. The humid air pressed on him as if a physical weight sat on his chest.

"If I have to marry a girl, Lyn, you know I want it to be you." He didn't know what else to say.

"Just what every girl wants to hear," Lyn muttered, her voice so low he almost didn't hear the comment. He frowned again. The two of them getting married was not news. Their fathers were business partners, and their parents, close friends for years, had been planning it since they were in diapers. It made sense to everyone involved, everyone except Lyn and Aaron.

The plan was simple. Aaron would graduate from high school with honors and then attend Harvard Business School. After graduating, he would marry Lyn. He would work in the family's shipping company until his father retired, when Aaron would take over. Lyn was expected to be the perfect society wife. They'd have children and play model family for the investors and clients. The plan was more than just "good business." It was a future born of their parents' friendship, which made it that much harder to reject.

"Look," Aaron said, "we'll be at the beach house in a few minutes, and then we'll have the next three months to enjoy ourselves. Let's not worry about the rest right now."

Lyn took a deep breath, as if she was going to say something else, but she just squared her shoulders and nodded.

"So, ready to lay out on the beach?"

"Please," he said. "You just use that as a chance to scope out the boys."

"It makes for a nice view." She smiled, and the tension seemed to dissipate. "You can't deny it."

"That it does."

Aaron's cheeks were tinged with red. Lyn giggled. Aaron's sexuality was something he'd only shared with Lyn. It was something that had come to light after too much champagne at a family party. It was a side of himself that he was still not quite comfortable with expressing, even with Lyn. His parents had no idea. The thought of telling them, of seeing their faces fall, of losing his family forever, was too much for him. Aaron couldn't do it.

Lyn tucked a loose strand of hair behind her ear with her left hand and Aaron imagined putting a ring on her third finger, trying once again to feel the joy that should come with such a thought. He couldn't quite manage it, no matter how hard he focused. The number of times he had tried was staggering.

He'd spent so much time wishing he could feel something other than friendship for Lyn. As if somehow that would make him want it. As if it would magically make him straight, make him in love with Lyn the way they both deserved. As if it would make his parents see him as anything more than just a means to an end.

As if.

They pulled up in front of their families' vacation home a few moments later. Aaron pushed his melancholy thoughts to the back of his mind. He would put them out of his head for the next few months and focus instead on having the best summer of his life. Lyn would be glad to hear that.

Aaron put the car in park, got out, and opened the door for her.

"Looks like we beat the parentals," Lyn said.

He grinned at her use of their nickname for all four of their parents. It was easier to refer to them that way, as they tended to travel in a unit. Lyn's favorite joke was that they shared a brain. Aaron couldn't disagree.

She smoothed her sundress as she rose, and her flip-flops slapped against the bottoms of her feet as she headed for the back of the car.

Aaron popped the trunk with a press of the button on his keychain. He handed Lyn her overnight bag. Gathering the remaining suitcases in his arms, he silently cursed Lyn's penchant to over-pack.

Trying not to groan under the weight of their suitcases, Aaron suppressed a sigh. "I'm sure they'll be here soon," he said. They hadn't been that far ahead of their parents. Besides, he knew better than to hope for things to go his way.

"So?" Lyn said. "It still gives us a head start down to the beach."

The steps they climbed were familiar, as was the white clapboard siding. He and Lyn had spent every summer in this house for over a decade. He knew every room like the back of his hand, even if his mother had redecorated since last summer. Given the number of rooms it contained, "house" wasn't quite the right name for the structure. Calling it a mansion was so pretentious, though. He didn't like the word. Lyn unlocked the front door and they went inside.

Their feet echoed on the hardwood flooring. The lemony smell of furniture polish tickled his nose as they went down the hallway. He and Lyn had had the same rooms in the house since they were kids. He always felt much more at home here than he did at their house in Savannah. Aaron inhaled; contentment washed over him.

In Lyn's room he set Lyn's luggage on her bed and she immediately dropped into a chair. Her room was simple: white walls, pink bedspread, and a vanity in the corner. It would be cluttered with makeup and jewelry before the night was out. None of it was Lyn's taste; she despised the color pink. She couldn't say anything, of course. Their mothers had decorated it for her last year and, as she did with most things her parents did, she had feigned joy at the gesture.

Aaron understood. It was easier that way.

He went to his own room and started to unpack. He relished the familiar blue walls; the nautical accents in the room were just the way he remembered. The décor was his attempt, no matter how futile, to bring the ocean indoors.

Aaron hoped that his clothes had travelled well. He checked them over. The last thing he wanted was to spend his first night on the beach ironing, but he would. The stir he would cause by showing up to dinner with a wrinkled shirt or slacks would be so much more unpleasant. Lyn knocked on his open door, already clad in her swimsuit.

He nearly bit his tongue in shock. Lyn was clad in one of the skimpiest bikinis he'd ever seen. Hell, he'd never even seen her in a two-piece before. Her parents were very firm about her wardrobe. The parentals were going to *freak*.

"Come on, slow poke," she told him, ignoring his obvious reaction. "Unpack later."

He could hear the sound of crashing waves through the open window. Aaron glanced down at the polo shirt in his hands, longing to hit the beach.

"Come on," she pleaded, dragging out the last word. "You know our parents will flip if I go down there without you."

"Fine." Aaron agreed and put the shirt down. They would freak, especially given her current state of dress. "But if my clothes wrinkle, you're ironing them."

He didn't need a reprimand from his parents the first night. She rolled her eyes at him but nodded. Aaron ducked into the bathroom, changed into his swimming trunks, and slathered on sunscreen. He was fair-skinned and didn't tan so much as burn to a crisp.

He and Lyn spent the rest of the afternoon on the beach sunning themselves. Aaron managed to drag Lyn into the water after much cajoling and promises that he wouldn't dunk her in the salty waves. Swimming relaxed him; Aaron had always loved the water. It muted the world around him, and no one expected anything from him when he was out in the water.

Lyn finally gave up on swimming and Aaron joined her on the beach a half hour later. He dried off with one of their oversize towels before stretching out to let the sun do its job. He slipped into a light slumber, but the ping of his phone receiving a text woke him.

"They're here," he said, and without words they packed up their things and set off, walking through the sand as quickly as they could manage. As they entered through the front door, Aaron could hear the clanging of pots and pans in the kitchen. Soft voices and gentle laughter reached his ears, and he took a deep breath. Leaving the beach items on the porch to air out, he and Lyn hurried up the stairs. Aaron changed as quickly as he could, putting on a soft blue polo shirt and a pair of khaki shorts. His clothes were not wrinkled, so Lyn was off the hook for ironing duty.

Having changed into a demure sundress, she joined him in the hallway. Her hair was pulled back with a barrette so that a few wispy strands framed her face. She was beautiful, aesthetically pleasing. Aaron just felt no sexual attraction to her whatsoever. They shared a knowing glance and pasted matching smiles on their faces. Her hand wrapped around his proffered elbow as he escorted her down the stairs and into the kitchen.

"Aaron, sweetie, there you two are," his mother said. Jennifer Ledbetter stood in front of the stove stirring a tomato-based sauce. Her soft, reddish-brown hair fell around her face.

"Sorry. Lyn and I lost track of time on the beach."

Jennifer tutted a gentle reprimand, and Aaron grimaced. He could only hope his father hadn't noticed. He did not want to sit through another hour-long lecture on the importance of punctuality.

"You kids are always out there first thing," Susan Rossman said. She was next to his mother, tossing together ingredients for a salad. Both women often employed a cook in the city, due to their social obligations and busy schedules. During the summer, though, his mother and Mrs. Rossman enjoyed doing their own cooking.

"Of course they are," Ronald Rossman said. "I'm sure Aaron here couldn't wait to get our Evie out on the beach." He elbowed Aaron's father in a knowing way. Aaron turned bright red at the innuendo: as if seeing Lyn in her bathing suit was the only reason he'd want to spend time on the beach with her.

Charles let out a chuckle as Aaron led Lyn over to a stool at the counter and held it for her as she sat down. Angry on his behalf and Lyn's, Aaron tried not to glare at them. She was more than just a pretty face with boobs. He wished he wasn't the only one who recognized that. He'd see it even if he weren't gay.

"Oh, don't tease them, Ronald!" Susan scolded, as she shook the salad tongs playfully in her husband's direction.

Aaron glanced at Lyn just in time to see her wince and then smooth her face into a neutral expression. He wasn't sure which part of that exchange had upset her more. He knew she hated it when her parents called her Evie, but the suggestion that she was nothing more than eye candy was also horrible. Aaron was glad the parentals had missed Lyn's new bathing suit. It would have put quite the capper on the current conversation.

It was shocking how good they were at hiding their real feelings. Aaron wasn't sure he'd expressed a true emotion in front his parents in years, unless he counted apologizing to them for not meeting the standards they'd set. He was pretty sure it had been even longer for Lyn.

Their fathers sat at the table, and it wasn't long before they were having a heated debate about something business-related. Aaron tuned them out, something he'd gotten really good at.

In an effort to avoid the conversation, Aaron went to the kitchen cabinets to grab plates as well as silverware and glasses. He didn't want to talk about business, like, ever, but definitely not now. It was summer. His mother kissed him on the cheek as he went past her, and handed Lyn the bowl of salad to take to the table. Aaron steeled himself, followed Lyn, and put down the plates and cutlery, knowing his plan had backfired thanks to his mother's subtle interference.

"Aaron, son, take a seat," his father said, ignoring Lyn although she was standing next to him. "We need your opinion on something."

He bit his lip and swallowed the urge to protest. He sat down in the closest empty chair. Lyn shot him a sympathetic look over her shoulder. Aaron forced himself to pay attention to the conversation and answer appropriately, earning a hearty pat on the back from his father. Joy welled up in him and he savored it. His father did not dole out compliments lightly.

Susan brought a large bowl of pasta to the table. "You know, kids, I was at the market earlier and there was a notice about a carnival in town this summer. It's set up near the pier."

"Oh, that sounds like a wonderful place for a date," Jennifer chimed in, and turned to look at Aaron and Lyn. "You two should make time to go there."

Aaron suppressed the urge to lean back when she focused her gaze on him. "I'm sure Evie would love for you to win her a stuffed animal."

"And I bet the view from the top of the Ferris wheel is spectacular at night," Susan added with a wink. Aaron's stomach sank. He caught Lyn's eye, and she nodded.

"Of course, Mother," Aaron agreed softly. Going to a carnival would be something both of them would love, if it wasn't being imposed upon them. "We can go tomorrow."

"It sounds like fun." Lyn said, her familiar false smile gracing her lips.

Aaron held in a sigh. He refused to let this get him down. He was going to enjoy this summer if it killed him.

* * *

LUCKY LET HIMSELF INTO THE trailer he'd be staying in for the summer. He was glad that it wasn't a tent. As much as he wanted an adventure this summer, he wasn't sure he wanted to give up four walls and a bed. A window air conditioner was going full blast, and Lucky let out a happy sigh.

"You must be Jonas," a gruff voice spoke up. Lucky turned around and his eyes widened as he took in the voice's owner: a man with a graying beard and a thicker southern accent than his own.

"Yeah," he replied, "But call me Lucky."

"I'm Bud." Lucky held out his hand but Bud ignored it. He pointed toward an empty bed. "That's your bed. That one's mine, and that one over there is Walter's."

Lucky nodded, tempted to ask where "Walter" was, but he didn't. He assumed that he'd meet the other man soon enough. It was a small trailer, there was no possible way Lucky would miss him.

"Best get some shut eye, kid," Bud continued, sitting on his bed. He directed his attention to a small TV on the nightstand. "It's gonna be a long day tomorrow, first day n' all."

Bud was obviously an experienced carnie, and Lucky thought he would be a fool not to listen. Besides, it didn't seem as though Bud was the small-talk type. Lucky quietly slipped into the bathroom to change and wash up from his trip. The hours on the bus had passed in a haze; he'd spent the time sleeping, sketching nothing but crap, and stretching his legs during walks to the tiny bathroom at the back of the bus.

By the time he came out of the bathroom, both beds held snoring men. Walter seemed to be younger than Bud but older than Lucky was. He put in his earplugs before slipping under the covers. He could hardly believe that he was finally there. He willed himself to relax, closing his eyes and rolling over onto his side.

Tomorrow would be a big day.

Chapter Two

AARON WRAPPED AN ARM AROUND Lyn's shoulders and pulled her close as they moved through the crowd. The carnival was definitely a popular attraction; they were bumping into people left and right. The whirring and clanking sounds of the rides and the screams of passengers were inescapable as Aaron led Lyn down the midway. They bought cotton candy to share and found a spot off the midway to sit. Aaron tried his best to eat the sweet treat without getting his hands sticky.

Lynn laughed. "You're worse than me."

"Now, now," Aaron teased, moving as if he was going to touch his sticky fingers to her face. "It wouldn't be becoming for a proper lady to end up with food on her face."

She glared at him and pulled a piece of the sugary floss loose. "You wouldn't dare." Lyn gave him a challenging look. He chuckled and licked his fingers. "Besides," she told him, "I'm no lady, and you look better in pink anyway."

She lunged at him with a piece of the sticky treat in her hand, aiming for his face. Aaron jerked backward just a second too late. Laughing along with her, he tried to wipe away the offending food from where it had adhered itself to his cheek.

"Yuck." Aaron glared at her playfully. "What would your mother say?"

Lyn shrugged. She grinned at him and shoved another bunch of cotton candy into her mouth.

"She's not here."

Aaron let out a laugh. When he glanced up, he spotted a men's restroom sign. "I'm going to go wash my face."

"Fine. More for me."

"I'm on to you, *Evelyn*," he teased, before heading for the bathroom. "And everyone thinks you're so proper."

Inside the bathroom, the sounds from outside were muffled, and the humidity nearly stole his breath away. Aaron washed his hands thoroughly and then dabbed lightly at his cheek with a dampened, soapy piece of paper towel. He noticed a guy about his age washing his hands in the sink next to him. The guy's eyes were wide, his mouth was hanging open just a little, and he was looking at Aaron as though Aaron had just done something extraordinary.

"I'm sorry, am I in your way?" Aaron asked, turning slightly. He couldn't remember the last time anyone, guy or girl, had looked at him in such a way. His skin prickled. He wasn't sure he liked it.

"Your profile is breathtaking," the guy said.

"Excuse me?" Whatever he'd expected the guy to say, it certainly wasn't that. He took a better look at the person next to him, noting the his light brown skin, his curly brown hair, his bright but surprisingly not tacky carnival uniform, and his beat-up sneakers.

"Your profile," the guy repeated, speaking slowly, as if Aaron was hard-of-hearing or a slow learner. It would have upset Aaron, if it weren't for the rapt expression still on the guy's face. "The way you look from the side."

"I know what a profile is." Aaron laughed, his cheeks flushed. He brushed his hair back from his face. "I'm just confused as to why you're commenting on mine while in the men's bathroom."

"Oh. Sorry." The guy glanced around as though he'd suddenly remembered where they were. The bashful expression on his face was endearing. "I'm an artist. I couldn't help but notice." He paused. "And I said so in the bathroom because that's where we happen to be. Didn't mean to freak you out."

Aaron couldn't imagine approaching a stranger in a bathroom the way this guy had. Too many years of being told to behave properly in public topped with a fear of being accused of trying to take a peek at another guy naked had made that something he would never consider doing. This guy apparently had no qualms about it.

"You didn't, and thanks, I guess," Aaron told him. His face was as clean as it was going to get.

"I'm Lucky." Aaron did a double take, and the guy let out a throaty chuckle. Shivers ran down Aaron's spine, and it was all he could do not to shudder. "My name is Lucky."

"Aaron Ledbetter," Aaron said, holding out his hand. Lucky took it, looking amused, and Aaron grimaced. Lucky probably assumed he was nuts. What teenager greeted another with a handshake? It had been so long since Aaron had met anyone outside his parent's circle of friends, he'd forgotten how to introduce himself to a normal guy. "It's nice to meet you."

"Back at ya," Lucky said.

Aaron floundered for something to say—there were no etiquette lessons on what to do when someone introduced themselves in the bathroom—and finally blurted out the first thing that came to him. "Your name is Lucky?"

He'd had every social faux pas drilled out of him over the years, except foot-in-mouth disease, it seemed. Lucky grinned, and Aaron squirmed in embarrassment.

"It's a nickname. Jonas is just so average, you know?" Aaron nodded, even though he wasn't sure anything about this guy could be considered average. "Listen," Lucky continued, "I'm working down at one of the booths, doing caricatures. I'd love to draw you, if you're interested."

"Uh, maybe." Aaron let go of Lucky's hand. His heart beat a little faster than usual, and he hoped Lucky couldn't hear it. That would be beyond mortifying, and that said something, considering their exchange so far.

"Awesome," Lucky said. "Well, I gotta go, I'm sure my break's over, and since I'm one of the new guys, I can't afford to be late. See you around."

"Yeah," Aaron said softly as Jonas left the bathroom. "See you."

He took a moment to pull himself together, unsure why he was so shaken from a two-minute encounter with a guy in the bathroom. Convincing himself that it had to be because of the heat, he went outside to find Lyn. They should find a drink stand; he evidently needed to cool off.

Lucky couldn't help the extra spring in his step as he headed back to his booth. He couldn't believe what had just happened. He'd met the world's cutest guy and in a *public bathroom*, of all places. He chuckled and shook his head as he turned the corner. His booth was at the end, near the pier. He loved the view of the ocean that it afforded him and he couldn't wait to see what it looked like at night, with the carnival lights in the background. He considered sketching that vision or perhaps even painting it, until Aaron's face made its way back into his head.

At his booth, Lucky took down the sign that said he was on break and sat beside his easel. His was a busy spot; the drawings were reasonably priced for a carnival, and people loved to see themselves as their favorite fictional characters. He and his booth partners also got tips, which they were allowed to keep at the end of their shifts—not a bad way to earn cash.

The rest of the afternoon, he replayed how delightfully flustered Aaron he had been when Lucky told him he wanted to draw him. It was true. The urge to grab a pencil and draw him was like an itch. Anytime he had that feeling, he was incredibly pleased with the results.

It had been a long time since he'd felt that spark. He toyed with the idea of drawing Aaron right then, but the arrival of a little girl and her stressed-out mother distracted him.

Lucky exhaled, put on a smile, and got to work.

Aaron found Lyn with a smile on her face, sitting at the table where he'd left her, tapping out something on her phone. He started to ask her who she was texting, but before he could get the question out, she glanced up at him and told him she was thirsty. He steered them toward a food cart, and after they'd slurped down a couple of sweet teas, they headed for the main attraction: the rides. Their options were standard carnival fare: a few rides that spun, a couple that went up in the air, a Ferris wheel, and bumper cars.

They exited the bumper cars, giggling like idiots. When Lyn slowed to a stop, Aaron nearly bumped into her. He stopped himself just in time.

"Lyn?" he asked. .

She stared at the booth to her right. Aaron followed her gaze and sucked in a deep breath.

"Lyn?"

"I want a tattoo."

"What?" Aaron said with a laugh.

"You heard me, Aaron."

"A tattoo?" He never in a million years would have expected that to come out of Lyn's mouth.

"Yes." Lyn nodded, emphasizing her tone. Aaron was speechless. Lyn wanted a tattoo. Next, pigs would fly. "And you're getting one too."

"No way." Aaron shook his head. "The parentals would flip."

"They don't have to know. We're eighteen. We need to start acting like it. "

"Tattoos are permanent, Lyn."

"That's the point, genius."

Aaron shook his head. Lyn liked to take chances, and she was more of a risk taker than he ever was, but this was a bit much, even for her.

Aaron imagined the look on his father's face if he came home with a tattoo. "No. And you shouldn't either."

"I don't need your permission, Aaron. You're not my father."

"Whoa, what—" He felt as if he'd been punched in the stomach. "I'm not your dad."

"Then stop acting like him. Come on," she pleaded.

"No." Aaron turned around and stopped short.

"What? Oh God, the parentals?"

"No." Aaron startled at the sight before his eyes. He'd momentarily forgotten about the boy from the bathroom. Lucky was right in front of them now, set up at a booth, drawing a boy seated in front of him. Aaron studied Lucky while he worked, taking in the squint of his eyes and how he absentmindedly brushed his hair out of his face when the wind blew it.

"What are you looking at?" Lyn asked.

"What?" Aaron glanced at her. "Oh, nothing."

She gave him a look that indicated she didn't believe him and opened her mouth to say something else when another voice rang out.

"Aaron!"

Aaron jerked his head back in Lucky's direction. The little boy was now gone. Lucky smiled at Aaron and waved.

"Nothing, huh?" Lyn gave him a pointed look. "Maybe I should have said 'who,' instead."

"He's just a guy I met in the bathroom," Aaron explained, flustered. Lyn's eyebrows shot up toward her hairline; her eyes widened. "Oh goodness, Lyn, not like *that*! He complimented me on my profile."

"Your *profile*?"

"Are you a parrot now?" he asked, trying not to snap. Aaron wasn't sure why the conversation unsettled him, but it did, and he just wanted to go somewhere else. He wanted to get away from Lucky and the feeling building up in his stomach.

"Nope." Lyn took him by the hand. "But I suddenly have a need to see us drawn as Fred and Wilma Flintstone."

Aaron opened his mouth to reply but was unable to get any words out before Lyn grinned and grabbed his hand. Despite his stuttered protest, she practically dragged him to Lucky's booth. He didn't want to talk to this guy again; looking at his beautiful smile and warm brown eyes had flustered Aaron as no one ever had, and he didn't like it.

"You came!" Lucky smiled brightly. His hair bounced wildly along with the rest of him, and Aaron found himself smiling back. It was hard not to copy Lucky's enthusiasm.

"Uh, yeah," Aaron replied, clinging to Lyn's hand. He'd never been in a situation remotely like this and he was at a complete loss for something to say. It was very clear to him that this was a terrible idea. The worst idea Lyn had ever had.

"And who is this lovely lady?" Lucky turned to look at Lyn.

"Oh, uh, this is my—this is Lyn." Aaron very nearly introduced Lyn as his girlfriend, a habit from years of social events together. But he didn't want Lucky to see her as his girlfriend.

"Evelyn Rossman," Lyn said, shooting Aaron an amused look. She was going to give him so much crap for this later. Goody. "You can call me Lyn."

Aaron's mouth fell open. Lyn was his pet name for her. She'd never, not once that he could recall, introduced herself as Lyn. He swallowed his comment.

"Jonas Luckett," Lucky told her. "But everyone calls me Lucky."

"Aaron said you wanted to draw him?" Lyn laced the question with innuendo. Aaron tried to pull his hand free then, but Lyn held tight.

"He's got a great profile," Lucky said.

"He has *lots* of great assets," Lyn said, in a teasing tone. Aaron's face flushed again as Lucky's questioning gaze met his. Lyn was milking this for all it was worth, making Aaron wish a hole would open up right there in the concrete and swallow him. He would have to find a way to make her pay for this later, if he didn't die from the humiliation first.

"*Lyn!*" he hissed at her. He wished that he was anywhere else. If only wishing worked, but, alas, he lacked the ability to make it happen.

Lucky gestured at the chairs behind them. "Why don't you two sit down? Now," he smiled as they settled, "what would you like me to draw for you?"

"Can you draw us as *The Flintstones*?" Lyn asked. Aaron still had no idea what it was Lyn loved about that silly cartoon series. She'd been obsessed with it since they were kids, once even attempting to dye her hair red like Wilma's. That had not gone over well with her parents, and her blonde hair had been restored before she could blink.

"I sure can," Lucky told her.

Aaron couldn't help staring as Lucky picked up a pencil and put it to the paper. He was mesmerized by Lucky's fingers as he made nimble strokes. Aaron had to force himself to look down every time Lucky glanced up at them, and left Lyn to carry most of the conversation. His face was tight and hot, as if he was getting sunburned; it radiated warmth and he wondered if it might become permanently red. Maybe his sunblock had come off when he washed his face. Lucky bit his lip in concentration, and Aaron bit back a gasp.

"There!" Lucky exclaimed, startling Aaron out of his reverie. "All done!"

He tore the sheet of paper from his pad and held up a picture of Aaron and Lyn as *The Flintstones*. "I love it!" Lyn said as she reached for it. "You're so talented."

"Thanks," Lucky replied.

"It's really good," Aaron said. "You should look into being an artist professionally, or something."

"That's the dream." Lucky smiled at him, and Aaron could have sworn his heart skipped a beat. "Thanks."

"Anytime," Aaron managed to get out.

Lyn nudged him. "Aaron, pay the man."

He'd been staring at Lucky again. He fumbled for his wallet. After checking the sign to see how much the picture cost, he handed Lucky a few bills. His fingers barely brushing against Aaron's, Lucky took the money. Aaron suddenly felt as if he couldn't breathe. He took a moment to get himself under control, spotting the tip jar in in the middle of the booth as he did so. When Lucky wasn't looking, Aaron slipped another bill into the jar.

"Thanks again, Lucky," Lyn said. She took their picture, which was now rolled up neatly and placed in a cardboard tube.

"Come back anytime," Lucky told them. "I'll be here all summer and I'd love to draw you again."

Aaron nodded and let Lyn lead him away from the booth. He stumbled through the crowd, unable to focus on anything. It was a good thing that Lyn had a grip on his arm; she had to steer him. They walked away from the carnival and headed along the beach in the twilight.

"What was *that*?" Aaron asked as soon as he recovered his ability to speak.

"What was what?" Lyn asked. With her blank expression and big eyes, she looked the picture of innocence.

Aaron glared at her. "Don't you dare, *Evelyn*/ You know exactly what I'm talking about."

"We're out in public, Aaron. I was being a loving girlfriend."

Aaron snorted and said, "Lucky thinks that we're together."

Lynn laughed. "*Oh*," she said, sounding delighted. He expected her to start bouncing up and down and clapping her hands as they walked. "It's finally happened."

"What has?"

"You *like* him," Lyn said, still laughing. "You like him a *lot*. You think he's pretty and you wanna marry him and have a million babies."

"I do not!"

"You do too!"

Aaron spluttered, searching for words in his panic. "I just met him!"

Lynn shrugged. "So? That's called attraction, Aaron. Pheromones, baby. Just admit that you think he's hot and you wanna get down and dirty with him," Lyn said, in a teasing tone, "and I won't say another word about it."

"*Lyn!*" Aaron sounded like a scandalized society mother, but he couldn't help it. He didn't want that because he *couldn't* want that. It wasn't part of The Plan. "I do not!"

"Uh huh." Lyn grinned. "Me thinks the dude doth protest too much."

Aaron growled. Sometimes Lyn was like a dog with a bone; she didn't know when to let things go.

"Well, even if you won't admit it, I can tell you one thing."

"What's that?" Aaron asked, half afraid of the answer.

"He was totally checking you out."

Aaron's mouth fell open. Other boys didn't check him out. They just didn't. "H-how do you know that?"

"Do I have to explain everything?" She shook her head. "You're hopeless, Aaron." The words were filled with affection, but he bristled at them. "And to think I had you pegged as having more affairs than me."

"*Lyn!*" he hissed. He couldn't believe they were having this conversation. If someone had told him this was how his day would end, he would have laughed. He was almost pinching himself as it was.

"That whole thing back there by the way, the way I was acting that you're so bent out of shape about?" she said, "that was me, putting my feelers out. I wanted to see if he was interested."

Aaron stopped in the middle of their yard and stared at her in shock.

"He wants you bad, sweetie." Lyn said. She patted him on the cheek and brushed past him with a triumphant smirk on her face. Aaron stared after her.

LUCKY DIALED HIS MOTHER'S NUMBER and lay back on his bed, glad his bunk mates were out. He had no idea where they were and it was nice to have some peace and quiet after the rush of the crowds all day. Reaching his mother's voicemail yet again, Lucky sighed. She was probably at work, but he'd hoped she might answer. He left a message letting her know how his first day had gone. He very nearly mentioned meeting Aaron, mostly because he wanted to talk about him with someone, but held back. She probably wouldn't want to hear it anyway. She'd tell him that he needed to focus on his job and honing his talent and that boys would be a distraction. That's what she'd told him over and over since he'd come out at fifteen.

Lucky's mind turned back to Aaron for the millionth time since that afternoon as he hung up the phone. Meeting Aaron, seeing him in the bathroom, was like lightening had struck. Lucky hadn't been kidding about Aaron's profile. He'd yet to meet a person who'd affected him as strongly Aaron had, one who made him want to put pencil to paper immediately. One who made his heart race and his skin tingle with the urge to create.

Aaron's friend Lyn was sweet and funny, and she was most likely his girlfriend, which meant Lucky needed to stop thinking about Aaron in that way. The last thing he wanted was to get hung up on a guy he couldn't have and distract himself from his art.

Yet, a face like Aaron's deserved more than just a quick sketch. Maybe he would live up to his nickname and bump into Aaron again soon. He tried not to hope for it.

So what if meeting Aaron had prompted an urge to draw that had eluded him for months? It didn't have to mean anything. Lucky tried to convince himself as he flipped passed his half-assed sketches from the bus trip. Lucky began to draw.

Chapter Three

"LAZY BONES! I LET YOU sleep long enough. Get a move on, I want to go out for lunch."

Aaron startled awake at Lyn's voice. He rolled over in bed, glanced at the clock and winced at the realization that he'd slept through breakfast. He'd been unable to sleep soundly the last few nights; he'd tossed and turned until all hours while Lyn's words about Lucky played on constant repeat in his mind.

Aaron spent the last week avoiding the carnival. Not that he'd let on about it to Lyn; she'd never let him hear the end of it. Instead, they'd spent the week sunbathing, snorkeling, and even rented a boat for a few hours. He'd tried everything he could to keep Lucky out of his head.

It had worked for the most part, until he climbed into bed. Once there, his mind would cease to be under his control, and he'd find himself analyzing Lucky's hair or smile, replaying their conversations, and hearing Lyn insist that Lucky was interested over and over.

He groaned.

For the first time in his life, Aaron wanted to tell Lyn to go eat by herself. He simply wanted to lay in bed, pull the covers over his head, and shut out the world. He wanted to stop wondering about things he couldn't have. But he couldn't brush Lyn off; the prospect of disappointing his parents was enough to propel him into motion.

"Give me twenty minutes," Aaron called as he forced himself to get up. He pushed Lucky out of his mind. What was the point of thinking about him? It would only lead to heartbreak and madness.

Lucky startled at the vibration in his pocket, and scrambled to dig out his phone. He glanced at the caller ID and answered it.

"Mama, hi."

"Hello, Jonas. How's it going?"

"Pretty good. I'm learning a lot about carnival life and I'm drawing so much I'm worried my fingers might fall off."

"Good boy," she said. "Soak up everything you can. It will give you an advantage in college."

"I will. You should try to get out here, take a vacation for once. The beach really is great."

"You know that's not possible. I have bills to pay and no time to run off and be foolish."

Lucky held back a sigh. He couldn't remember the last time his mother had done anything resembling fun.

"You work too hard, Mama." The words slipped out even though they wouldn't do any good. His mother had been working herself exhausted since he could remember and maybe before that.

"Don't worry about me. You know I do what has to be done."

Lucky changed the subject, launching into a story about a drawing he'd done the other day, hoping he could make her laugh. Talking about his drawings led to him thinking about Aaron though, and before he knew it, he was telling his mother about drawing Aaron and Lyn.

"What do you know about this boy?" The intensity in her voice startled him.

"What?"

"I hear it when you talk about him," Dinah said. "You're interested in him."

"Mama, I barely know him. I haven't seen him since anyway. You're reading too much into things."

"You stay away from boys, Lucky. You're there to make money for school, and learn."

"I *know*, Mama."

Lucky endured more advice and criticisms from his mother until he managed to wind up the conversation. After they hung up, he flung himself backward on his bed and stared at the ceiling. He hated that his mother was so closed off sometimes. Just once, he wanted to giggle and gossip with her about boys.

It would be nice to have someone to talk to about everything. His friends back home had gone off to bigger and better things or were working, like him. The infrequent texts or calls were summaries of their lives rather than anecdotes and gossip. Lucky considered finding one of his roommates and confiding in them, but he dismissed the idea. Walter was nearly three time his age and barely spoke two words when he was in the trailer. Bud, on the other hand, was chatty, but brusque.

He sighed, glancing at his watch. It was early and he had the day off. He needed to get his mind off of… everything.

He had to get out of there.

Aaron sighed with relief as he and Lyn slid into a booth at the Magic Shore restaurant. He perused the menu to see if they had added any new dishes since the previous year. Their waitress stopped and took their orders. Aaron's stomach growled and he silently urged the kitchen staff to hurry.

Aaron nearly did a double take at the sight of Lucky sitting at a nearby table. Almost as if Lucky could feel his gaze, he glanced up and caught Aaron's eye. Aaron's face felt hot and he quickly glanced away. After spending the week avoiding him, Aaron could hardly believe that Lucky was just feet away.

"You're not even listening to me, are you?" Lyn's voice broke through his fog.

Aaron turned his head. "Of course I am."

"What did I just say?" she said. Aaron panicked. "That's what I thought. So what's more important than me?"

Lyn looked around the restaurant. The moment she spotted Lucky, her lips curved into a knowing smile. She made a little noise that sounded far too delighted to Aaron's ears.

Aaron suddenly found his glass of sweet tea very interesting and studied the condensation as it slid down the glass and made a ring of water on the tabletop. He wished the waitress would come back with their food and save him from whatever Lyn was planning. Her mischievous expression meant she was up to no good.

"Lucky!" Lyn called, waving. Aaron's stomach did a somersault, and he gave Lyn a look that should have killed her, if only looks could kill. He just wanted a quiet lunch and a swim before camping out under the beach umbrella to catch up on much-needed sleep. He didn't know why she wanted to push him on Lucky. What was the point?

Lucky looked up when Lyn called his name and returned her wave. Before Aaron could stop her, she went to Lucky's table. Aaron sucked in a breath; he was unable to find words when Lyn came back with Lucky in tow. She practically pushed him into the booth next to Aaron, then sat herself.

"Lucky's going to join us," she said, looking proud of herself. Aaron hadn't known he could clench his jaw that tightly.

"Hi," he managed to get out, glancing at Lucky. He could feel heat from Lucky's body and he was overwhelmed by it. If he moved his leg a fraction of an inch, they'd be touching. The idea made his head spin and his mouth go dry.

"Hi," Lucky said. Their eyes locked, and Aaron blushed again. He couldn't do this. Why was Lyn making him do this?

"I d-didn't expect to s-see you here," Aaron stammered. Why did he turn into a babbling idiot around Lucky? He was Aaron Ledbetter, for goodness' sake! He'd charmed more society men and women than he could count, but Lucky seemed to strike him dumb.

Lucky smiled at him. "I thought I'd sample the local fare. Carnival food gets old fast. You can only eat so many deep fried foods."

Their waitress arrived, bringing their food along with Lucky's. Aaron nibbled on a fry; his earlier hunger was dissipated by Lucky's nearness. The conversation launched into the worst deep-fried carnival foods Lucky had seen in years working for carnivals. As Lucky talked, Aaron started to relax. He even chuckled at Lyn's grossed-out faces.

Lyn swallowed a bite of her grilled chicken salad, then said, "So, Lucky, tell us about yourself. Where are you from?"

"Austin, Texas," Lucky answered before taking a bite of his fish sandwich. That explained Lucky's twang. Aaron loved the way Lucky spoke. Lucky chewed and swallowed before continuing. "I'm spending the summer with the carnival to make money for school in the fall. I'm going to SAIC, the School of the Art Institute of Chicago. It's one of the top three art schools in the country. "

"Wow, that's impressive," Lyn told him.

"You're really good," Aaron added before he could stop himself. Lucky's eyes met his again, and his stomach did a somersault. "At art, I mean."

"Thanks," Lucky replied, his cheeks tinged pink. Aaron stared. Had he caused that reaction? He stuffed a few more fries in his mouth before he said something else ridiculous.

"How did you discover your love for art?" Lyn asked, sipping her sweet tea.

"I was always drawing and coloring when I was younger," Lucky said, "and my art teacher in middle school was always willing to work with me on new styles and techniques. I just got hooked and kept at it as I got older."

Aaron hung on Lucky's every word, hoping that it wasn't obvious to either Lucky or Lyn.

"So what about you two?" Lucky changed the subject. "Any college plans?"

"Harvard Business School," Aaron said. It was the only answer, unless he wanted to disappoint his parents. His stomach clenched and he forced the feeling away by taking another bite.

"Wow," Lucky replied. "Congrats." Aaron nodded woodenly. "What about you, Lyn?"

"Not in the cards," Lyn demurred. A pang of sadness went through Aaron at the fake smile Lyn had pasted on her face. Lyn had wanted to go to college, but her parents hadn't seen it as necessary. That meant, of course, she wouldn't be going. She would spend her time abroad with their mothers, attending finishing school courses, and eventually planning their sure to be lavish and over the top society wedding.

It was enough to make Aaron scream but he held it in.

"That's cool," Lucky said. "College isn't for everyone."

"Right." Lyn's voice was stiff. Her phone beeped, indicating she had a text. She texted a reply, and Aaron took the moment to stare discreetly at Lucky.

"So, what's it like working at the carnival?" Aaron asked.

"Exhausting, mostly," Lucky said. "But it's also incredibly fun and I meet all kinds of fascinating people." Lucky's eyes met Aaron's as he spoke. Was Lucky implying...? Aaron shook his head. Even if, it didn't matter. He had Lyn, and his whole future was planned. "I'm rooming with these two guys who've been carnies since before I was born. It's kind of amazing."

Another text tone rang out in the momentary silence, and Lucky glanced at his phone. He read the text and frowned.

"Well, this has been fun, but I've just been called into work. The artist I share the booth with apparently decided that five corn dogs and the tilt-a-whirl made a good combination." Lyn shuddered and scrunched up her nose. Lucky laughed, then left a few dollars tip for the waitress.

"Hopefully we'll see you around!" Lyn told him, and Aaron nodded. Lucky flashed them a smile as he took his check up to the register. Aaron's breath caught in his throat—no one should look that good.

"You okay?" Lyn asked. She had a knowing expression, and he didn't like that at all. He stood up, pulled out several bills, and put them on the table.

"I have to go," he mumbled. He made his way to the exit, hoping she wouldn't tell their parents that he left her there. They would flip. Leaving the diner, he wished he could move even faster.

Aaron headed down the pier, dodging the crowd of sightseers. At the end of the pier, he found an empty bench and collapsed. He let the crash of the ocean waves, the drumbeat of the crowd, and the cries of the birds distract him.

"Hey." Lyn's voice was soft in his ears, and he turned to find her sitting beside him. She wore a concerned expression.

"I'm fine," he told her quietly. "I just..."

"I get it," Lyn said. He smiled at her; if anyone understood how he was feeling, it would be her. "It's okay to like him, you know."

"Who?" Aaron suddenly found his fingers fascinating. Aaron wanted something for the first time in years and *he couldn't have it*. He couldn't have Lucky. He couldn't talk about it. Talking about it would make it real, would make it hurt more.

Lyn was silent, refusing to play his game. Aaron sighed. She was going to force him to do this.

"Is it okay to like him?" he said, unable to keep the fear out of his voice.

"Yes." Lyn's tone was firm. "It is."

"But what's the point, Lyn?" Aaron stared out at the vast ocean. "I'll be gone after this summer, and Lucky and I will never see each other again. Besides," Aaron lowered his voice and spoke slowly, keeping his tone even to hide the dread swelling inside him as he continued, "you and I are getting married."

"I haven't forgotten," she replied softly, after a long minute. "The point is, Aaron, you'll regret it if you don't do something. Do you want to go through your life always wondering what could have been?" Lyn kissed his cheek and then got up. "Think about it."

Aaron remembered Lucky's smile, the way his hair fell in his eyes when he was drawing, his easygoing nature, and his seeming lack of fear. Aaron had met Lucky only a week ago, and already he was so drawn in. He couldn't remember ever feeling like this about someone. Sure, he'd appreciated other guys' looks in the past, but he'd never done anything about it. All of them had assumed he was with Lyn, and there seemed to be no point in trying to make it something more.

He groaned. This whole thing was insane. He barely knew Lucky. And yet Lyn's voice echoed in his head, telling him it was okay to want this, to want Lucky.

Maybe she was right. Maybe he owed it to himself to have this... fling, to get it out of his system. He made a deal with himself, then and there: *I'll see where this thing with Lucky goes, come hell or high water. Knowing my luck, probably both.*

Chapter Four

Alone in the house, Aaron spent the day vibrating from nerves. Their mothers had shanghaied Lyn for a shopping trip and their fathers went golfing. He'd been expected to go along but had begged off, claiming he didn't feel well. The lie hadn't set well; it turned in his stomach and made him feel ill. He couldn't stand disappointing his parents, even over something as trivial as not wanting to go golfing.

He'd ignored Lyn's questioning glance as she left and waited until everyone was gone to get out of bed and dressed. Now, as he nibbled on a piece of toast, he tried to shake off his guilt. Eager to see Lucky, he headed to the carnival. It had taken a few days for Aaron to get his nerve up, but now that he had, he had to act before he talked himself out of it.

He didn't head for Lucky's booth right away. He dawdled along the main strip, stopped to play a few games, and got a Coke from a food stand. Before he knew it though, Aaron came to a stop in front of Lucky's booth. There was no line and Aaron floundered, unsure what to do. He'd counted on a line of customers giving him time to come up with something to say; maybe he'd get to watch Lucky draw before having to rely on conversation.

"Aaron?" Lucky's voice penetrated the fog in his brain, and Aaron jerked his head up.

"Hmmm?" Aaron managed, distracted by Lucky's smile yet again.

"Did you want another drawing?"

"What? Um, yeah." His cheeks were probably bright red.

"Great! Want anything special?"

"Um, no," Aaron said. "Just... whatever you're inspired to draw."

Lucky nodded, urged Aaron into the chair at his booth, and put his pencil to the paper. Yet again, Aaron tried his best not to stare, at Lucky while he worked, but he wasn't successful.

"At least you didn't tell me to draw you like one of my French girls," Lucky said after a second, and Aaron gaped at him. Lucky chuckled and glanced up at him. "You wouldn't believe how often I get that."

If anyone else had said it, it probably would have come across as arrogant or self-centered, but the words were matter-of-fact and almost endearing coming from Lucky. "People actually say that?"

"All the time. Some people say it because they think they're clever or funny. Sometimes girls say it because they're hitting on me."

"Oh?" Aaron's hopes plummeted. He'd been so sure that Lucky was gay; Lyn had been certain Lucky had been checking him out. Had he come this far just to set himself up for misery? He wanted to run away, to hide somewhere until this feeling in his chest disappeared and he could get back to his life's plan.

"Yeah," Lucky grinned. "Never does them any good though." He paused, squinting at Aaron. "Not on their team."

Aaron didn't know his heart could actually skip beats, but he swore it happened at Lucky's words. Lucky was gay. His hope soared right alongside his nervousness.

Lucky put down his pencil and held up the paper for Aaron to see. Aaron's breath caught in his throat. The drawing was simple, but the expression on Aaron's face was pensive and uncertain, clearly not the caricature that Aaron had been expecting. Is that how he really seemed?

"I love it, thank you," Aaron murmured.

Lucky rolled up the picture and put it in a cardboard tube. Aaron pulled out his wallet to pay, and Lucky held up a hand to stop him.

"Don't," Lucky said quietly. "This one's on me."

"Are you sure?"

"Completely. Drawing you is always a pleasure."

"Right." Aaron's eyes locked with Lucky's. "I have a good profile."

"Among other things," Lucky agreed softly, his tone sending shivers down Aaron's spine.

Aaron clutched the cardboard tube; words escaped him.

Lucky glanced at his watch. "I'm due for a lunch break in a second. Wanna grab some food?"

"Sure." Aaron waited while Lucky turned the booth over to another guy. Aaron presumed he was the one who'd thought corn dogs and spinning rides was a good idea. Lucky then leapt over the booth's counter to stand in front of Aaron; the motion made Aaron's breath stop.

"What should we eat?" Lucky asked as they made their way past several food trucks.

Aaron shrugged, still struggling with words. "Surprise me."

"Okay." Lucky grinned. "Wait here, I'll be right back."

Aaron smiled back as Lucky went to a truck that sold some of the deep-fried concoctions he'd mentioned at the restaurant. Aaron shuddered. He could not eat that.

"As long as it's not deep fried!" Aaron called after him. Lucky turned around with a laugh.

"Spoil sport!" he shouted back. Lucky veered over to a pizza truck.

They found a secluded spot to sit, scarfed down pieces of pizza, and people-watched. Lucky put Aaron at ease. He had that way about him.

"I've got a few minutes left," Lucky said when they finished their food.

They got up, sipping at their drinks as they made their way through the crowd back toward Lucky's booth. It was now or never. He had to ask, had to get the words out, or miss his shot.

"Can I ask you something?" Lucky spoke up before Aaron could. Maybe Lucky would… Aaron held his breath, nodding. "It might sound weird."

"Sure." Aaron's heart beat a little faster. What could Lucky possibly want from him? A kiss?

"Can you take your picture for me?"

Aaron blinked at him. Lucky tilted his head and Aaron turned his head the same direction. His gaze landed on a photo booth, realization sinking in. His mouth fell open, unsure what to say. It was weird because they barely knew each other, but also flattering.

"I'd really like to draw you again." Lucky looked at his shoes. "I mean, I could take pictures on my phone if that's better for you, but that seemed creepier somehow."

Aaron couldn't help but chuckle, even as the idea of Lucky drawing him again and again left him breathless. "Um," he managed to get out, glancing around at the crowd. A familiar blonde head caught his eye, and he nearly choked.

Was Lyn at the carnival? Wasn't she supposed to be with their mothers?

Aaron pulled Lucky by the hand into the photo booth and shut the curtain.

Lucky slid money into the slot as they sat. Aaron's breath caught as Lucky's hands touched his face gently. "Like this," Lucky whispered, turning his head to the side. The camera flashed. Lucky's fingers turned Aaron's head to the front, pulling away just before the camera clicked again. Once again, Lucky's fingers turned Aaron head to the side, only now he faced Lucky. Aaron tried not to hyperventilate as he held Lucky's gaze. The camera flashed for the last time, but neither of them moved.

"Go out with me?" Aaron blurted. He had to say something or he might do something even more insane, like kiss Lucky. Aaron so wasn't ready for that yet. Lucky's eyes widened and he smiled.

"Sure," Lucky drawled. "When?"

Aaron's mind worked quickly. The parentals were going into the city the next night for some charity event. They'd be gone most of the night, leaving him and Lyn to their own devices. He was sure he could find a way to get out of the house and away from Lyn. "Tomorrow night?"

"I get off at five," Lucky told him as they climbed out of the booth. Aaron glanced around and saw no sign of any familiar blonde heads. "We could go for dinner at the Magic Shore, at six?"

"See you then," Lucky said with a smile.

"See you," Aaron mumbled, turning to walk away. He kept his feet moving until he was sure Lucky could no longer see him. Then he stopped in his tracks, bent over and put his head between his knees to keep from passing out. He was nearly trampled by a woman with three kids who had been walking behind him, but he barely heard her cursing.

Aaron tried to regulate his breathing. He'd just asked another boy out on a date.

He'd just asked *Lucky* on a date and Lucky said *yes*.

Lucky said yes.

He could feel the ear-splitting grin spread as the reality of that set in. "Oh, my God."

LUCKY COULD HARDLY CONTAIN HIS smile as Aaron disappeared into the crowd. A boy had asked him out on a date. Not just any boy, *Aaron*. Aaron, who was clearly not straight because he had just asked Lucky *out on a date* and Lucky still couldn't quite believe it. His legs felt rubbery. He sank into his chair.

He was going out on a date with Aaron.

The rest of the afternoon he could hardly focus on work; his mind was full of Aaron. Fantasies of kept creeping in: holding Aaron's hand, kissing him. Lucky didn't think the customers really cared, as long as he managed passable drawings in response to their requests. It was all he could do not to give in to the itch in his fingers, the one that got under his skin until he had to draw the image in his head and put

Aaron's likeness on paper one more time. The strip of photos in his pocket did nothing to curb his desires.

He drew nearly constantly until the end of his shift. He was happy to turn his booth over to the other artist, now forever labeled in Lucky's mind as "corndog guy," and head back to his trailer as night fell.

"You swallow something, boy?" Bud's gruff voice reached his ears.

"*What?*" Lucky asked, staring at Bud. Bud was stretched out on his bed; his little TV droned on about a baseball team Lucky couldn't identify.

"You look like the cat that went and got the canary," Bud replied, never taking his eyes from the TV set.

"Oh, well, it's something like that, I guess."

Lucky was out and proud but not to his roommates. He almost never came face-to-face with Walter and he wasn't sure what to make of Bud, so telling them he was gay was difficult; there was no way to tell how people would react when they learned the truth, especially men from Bud and Walter's generation. He didn't want to spend the rest of his summer avoiding his roommates or worrying they might get him fired or even hurt him.

It sucked that these were legitimate fears, but they were always a possibility.

"She got a name?"

Lucky swallowed hard, debating and hating himself.

"Yeah," he managed to get out, hoping this did not go badly. "He does." There was a pause, and then Bud grunted. Lucky prayed that would be the end of the conversation. He flopped onto his bed and rolled over to face the wall before anything else could be said.

Aaron's joy lasted until he got home; everyone was there, waiting for him. They were dressed up as if they were going out to dinner, and Aaron swallowed hard. Oh, *crap*.

"Oh, Aaron, there you are!" his mother exclaimed. "We've been calling you for the last forty-five minutes."

Double crap.

"I'm so sorry. I was wandering around the carnival." He glanced at the cardboard tube in his hand. "I must not have heard it ring."

He'd turned his phone off so that nothing would disturb his time with Lucky. He had no desire to turn it back on now; the sheer number of phone calls and texts would probably do him in, given his current emotional state.

"We're having dinner with the Petermans, they're down here for the summer as well," Aaron's father informed him. "They were expecting us a half hour ago."

Aaron bit his lip and nodded; another apology left his lips as he rushed upstairs. The Petermans were an important client of the family business, and both sets of parents had to be upset with him. He flew through getting ready and was downstairs in under fifteen minutes.

The drive to the restaurant was quiet, with Lyn giving him concerned looks when she thought he wasn't paying attention.

He could hear John Peterman's voice the moment they stepped into the restaurant; the man's boisterous laugh echoed. Lyn's grip on his arm was tight as they walked to the table. Neither of them was fond of the man; he was ultra-conservative and extremely sexist, as well as homophobic. His son Richard wasn't much better in Aaron's eyes, a complete stick-in-the-mud who never once disagreed with his father. He was everything that Aaron was supposed to be. Aaron could have hated him for that alone. He steeled himself.

Their parents had made it clear that having a CEO who was different would not fly well with investors or clients. That meant he would never be able to come out. He told himself he was okay with that. If he couldn't bring himself to tell his parents, he certainly wasn't about to broadcast it.

"And here's the young man now!" John said as they reached the table. "Would have thought that pretty little thing on your arm would have been the holdup instead of you, boy." He elbowed his son in the ribs and Richard laughed.

Aaron's face grew warm, but he held his tongue. Lyn smiled demurely at the man, but Aaron was sure she was boiling with rage. He would hear all about it later.

"So sorry, sir. I lost track of the time," he finally managed to get out. He went to hold Lyn's chair—years of doing had ingrained that courtesy—only to be startled as Richard Peterman beat him to it.

"You better work on that, son, if you're going to run this company one day. Can't have a CEO who isn't on time," John said, giving him a hard look.

"Yes, sir," Aaron agreed. He took his seat next to Lyn and tried not to shrivel up under Mr. Peterman's stare. Lyn grabbed his hand under the table and squeezed it. Aaron shot her a grateful smile and hoped his disinterest in the conversation around him wouldn't show.

He spent the meal thinking about Lucky and wishing he was somewhere, *anywhere*, else. Lyn had to nudge him more than once; one time she even kicked him in the ankle. He did notice that she was speaking more with Richard than she'd ever bothered to before. That was strange, but Aaron let the idea of Lucky distract him before he could focus on it. Only Lyn seemed to be aware of his lack of attention. It was a relief to be able to contribute to the conversation occasionally despite hardly listening to it.

He was glad when the meal was over; putting on his facade was exhausting. Aaron wondered how he'd been doing it for so long.

"Where were you today?" Lyn asked after they said good night to their parents and headed upstairs for bed.

"At the carnival," Aaron replied. "Like I said earlier."

"Alone?"

Aaron let out a laugh, hoping it didn't sound too strained. He was bursting to tell her that he had actually asked Lucky out on a date, but something held him back. He wanted to keep it to himself for a bit, revel in it a little without Lyn putting in her two cents. And if things between him and Lucky didn't work out, then he wouldn't have to worry about what she would say.

"Who else would I go with? My best girl was working out with her AmEx card."

Lyn rolled her eyes and whacked him playfully on the arm. He must have been wrong thinking she was at the carnival. It was stupid of him, really. It was summer on the coast of Georgia; there had to be a million blonde girls milling about. Aaron chalked it up to his guilty conscience. She would have told him if she'd gone to the carnival. He stepped into his room with a quiet good night and shut the door behind him.

He sat on the edge of his bed; guilt at lying to Lyn pooled in his stomach. He took a deep breath and let out, hoping Lyn wouldn't bring it up again. Aaron lay back, put his hands under his head, and stared up at the ceiling as though it held all the answers. His thoughts turned to the next night, and how he'd get himself out of the house for his date. He hated to admit it, but he would lie to Lyn again if it meant seeing Lucky.

Lucky was worth it.

Aaron was almost asleep when he heard a soft knock. He immediately stiffened. Only one person knocked that way.

His father.

Almost falling out of bed in his haste to answer the door, Aaron choked back the rising panic. Charles Ledbetter was on the other side, just as Aaron knew he would be.

"Father, come in," Aaron said, stepping back to allow his father in the room. His father took three steps inside and motioned for Aaron to close the door.

Aaron tried to control his anxiety. His father was probably just concerned that he'd been late. He couldn't know about Lucky.

He couldn't.

"You were late today," his father said in a firm, disapproving voice.

"I know, I'm sorry, it won't happen again."

"It was rude and inconsiderate, Aaron."

"Yes, sir," Aaron whispered, staring at the floor.

"Over the years, I've done my best to accept your limitations, son, but this was beyond that."

"I'll write the Petermans a note of apology," Aaron rushed out.

"Not good enough," Charles said. "Richard will have dinner here one night soon." His father turned to the door and opened it slowly. "Be sure that you're on time."

Aaron nodded, sinking onto the edge of his bed. What has he doing? He didn't know anymore.

All he knew was that sleep wasn't going to come easily.

Chapter Five

Aaron woke to an empty house. He couldn't believe his luck—their fathers had gone into town for a business brunch. In all the years their families had been coming to the beach, their fathers had never seemed to grasp the concept of "vacation." According to the text she'd sent him, their mothers had dragged Lyn off for a spa day, which meant he had the entire day to himself to freak out about his date with Lucky.

He had to keep himself busy, so he grabbed a book and headed to the beach. After slathering up with sunscreen, he planted himself on the sand and tried to get lost in the book. It worked for a bit, but eventually Aaron found himself distracted; thoughts of Lucky and their upcoming date made concentrating difficult.

What should he wear? What should he should say? He pictured Lucky holding his hand, leaning in for a kiss. Aaron's stomach flipped over at the idea of finally knowing what it would be like to kiss another boy.

Aaron tried to keep his mind on Lucky and not his parents as he headed inside to shower and get ready. He needed to be gone before anyone got back because there was no way he could justify spending time outside the house with anyone else if Lyn was home. Neither set of parents would be willing to let him go out without her. As he got dressed, Aaron pushed back the nausea that seemed to hit any time he disobeyed his parents.

Aaron brushed his hair and stared at his reflection in the bathroom mirror. "You can do this," he murmured. "You can. Do what *you* want for once."

The restaurant was a short walk down the beach, and Aaron enjoyed the sun shining on him. He tried to keep his emotions in check, but he was coming apart at the seams; so many emotions swirled through him at one time. He'd had no idea it was possible to feel this much without exploding.

Nerves took over as he neared the diner and the smell of food reached his nose. He glanced through the windows and spotted Lucky inside, already sitting at a table. His mouth went dry. Lucky was wearing a black T-shirt and jean shorts, so different from the carnival uniform. Lucky's hair seemed wilder, if possible, and Aaron glanced down at himself. His polo shirt and khaki shorts would have blended perfectly at the local country club but seemed out of place when sharing space with Lucky.

Aaron forced himself to take a deep breath and made his way to the table where Lucky was sitting. He hoped Lucky liked men with red faces, because it seemed that blushing was his permanent state around the man.

"Hi," Aaron said.

Lucky glanced up from his intense study of the menu and smiled at him. "Hi."

Aaron slid slowly into the seat across from him and swallowed.

He couldn't do this.

"First date?" Lucky asked him. "You look like a deer caught in the headlights."

"That obvious, huh?" Aaron shook his head, smiling ruefully.

"A little," Lucky said, but Aaron was pretty sure Lucky was just saying that. "You're adorable, you know that?"

"I was... unaware." *Is this really happening?* A guy just told him he was adorable. An awkward silence fell over the table. He wasn't any good at this. He'd never had to figure out how to talk to anyone in a setting like this because he'd always had Lyn; she had been his date for every event and social function since he was twelve years old.

The waitress came to take their drink orders.

Aaron perused the menu, glad to have something for his hands to do. "The fish sandwich I had the other day was really good," Lucky said.

Aaron glanced up at him. "Oh?" He'd eaten at the diner many times; he had had the fish sandwich so often that he'd lost count, yet Lucky suggesting it made him want to have it. "I'll try that then."

The waitress took his order, and Aaron couldn't take his eyes off Lucky as he ordered a hamburger and fries. He averted his gaze when Lucky looked up and took a sip of his iced tea. Aaron's thoughts raced a mile a minute. He should say something, right? Because if he didn't it could get awkward, and he really wanted this date to go well.

"Do you and Lyn come up here every summer?" Lucky asked.

"We do. Our families are close and we vacation together every year."

"Must be nice to have a whole summer at the beach."

"It's my favorite part of the year," Aaron told him. "I love the beach and the tourists. It's nice to get lost in the crowd." Lucky was looking at him intently, and Aaron stopped there. If he went any further, he'd be getting into things he didn't want to talk about.

Conversation shifted to their childhoods and Aaron learned that Lucky was the only son of a single mother, who worked two jobs to put food on the table. Aaron didn't know how to relate to that, but Lucky either didn't notice or was too polite to point that out.

Aaron told Lucky a little about his family, too, but left out anything that he thought wasn't first date material. Aaron had no idea how to explain his family situation. He didn't want to chase off the first guy he was truly interested in by revealing he was still in the closet.

Once their food arrived, Aaron asked, "What do you love about art?"

"There's so much beauty in the world," Lucky said between bites, "but sometimes it seems like the bad things are the most common. Sometimes the only way I can deal with what I'm feeling when I see those things—beauty or sadness—is to draw them."

Aaron laughed when Lucky talked about how he'd done one season of powder-puff cheerleading through a league at a local recreation center. His mother had been livid when she'd found out, according to Lucky, but Aaron couldn't get the picture of Lucky in the uniform out of his mind to focus on that part of the story.

"So wait, the guys were wearing the cheerleading uniforms and the girls were the football players?"

"Yep," Lucky said, his eyes twinkling.

"Please tell me there are pictures," Aaron said. The idea of Lucky's slender frame in a skirt blew his mind.

"Let's just say the skirts left little to the imagination." That description didn't help Aaron's mental state and he was sure his face was bright red again.

The waitress put the check on the table. "I'll take this when you're ready," she told them, walking away with her ponytail bouncing. Aaron reached for the check, but Lucky beat him to it.

"My treat," Lucky insisted, pulling out his wallet.

"But I asked you."

Lucky still wouldn't hear of it, handing money and the check to the waitress before Aaron could stop him.

"Fine then," Aaron said, his tone slightly petulant. "Dessert is on me."

Lucky grinned and rose from his chair. "Lead the way."

After a glance at his phone to check the time, Aaron steered them toward the house. No one would be back yet. He was startled when Lucky suddenly took the device out of his hands.

"What are you doing?" he said.

Lucky pushed several of the phone buttons and then handed it back to him. "Saved you the trouble of asking for my number." Lucky said. "What's a guy gotta do to get yours?"

"Oh." Aaron reached for Lucky's phone; his fingertips buzzed when they brushed against Lucky's. He entered his number and then handed the phone back to Lucky, hoping Lucky wouldn't notice his shaking fingers.

At the house, Lucky slowed down, staring up at it.

"Nice house," he said.

Aaron shrugged. He hoped it didn't put Lucky off; he never wanted to make Lucky feel out of place just because Aaron had money. When Lucky didn't say anything further, Aaron directed him to a patio chair at the table on the porch. Aaron darted into the kitchen for the pint of vanilla ice cream in the freezer.

"Dessert!" he exclaimed, heading back outside with the pint of ice cream in one hand and two spoons in the other. Lucky laughed.

"Vanilla," Lucky said as Aaron took off the lid and sat next to him. "Why am I not surprised?"

"What's that supposed to mean?"

"It's just very *you*." Lucky swiped some ice cream from his spoon and dabbed it on Aaron's nose.

"Hey!" Aaron protested. Lucky laughed. His thumb trailed over the sticky liquid on Aaron's nose as he wiped it away. Aaron took a deep breath and inhaled the smell of Lucky's spicy cologne, He couldn't move; his eyes were locked on Lucky's mouth. He closed his eyes as Lucky moved closer. His heart beat rapidly. This was it. He was going to get his first *real* kiss. Years of chaste pecks with Lyn did not count.

The front door opened suddenly, the sound like a gunshot in the night. The sound of voices reached the patio. Aaron's eyes shot open and he practically jumped out of his chair.

"You have to go!" he whispered.

Why had he assumed he could do this? He couldn't do this. Lucky had to go and he had to go *now* or *everything* would be ruined.

Lucky gave him a long look, seeming startled by his forceful tone.

"Please," Aaron pleaded, with a fearful glance at the back door. All it would take was one of them to step outside…

"Okay," Lucky said.

Lucky stared at Aaron for a few tense moments, then disappeared into the darkness. Aaron ran his hands through his hair and took several deep breaths in an effort to get himself back under control. The spoons clanked together as he gathered them and slapped the lid back on the pint of ice cream before heading inside. Lyn was in the kitchen taking a bottle of water out of the refrigerator.

"How was the spa?" he asked, opening the freezer door and shoving the pint back inside. He'd eat it later, once his stomach stopped turning somersaults.

"Invigorating." Lyn took a drink of water. "What did you do today?"

"Hung out on the beach and read, mostly."

"Ah."

"What?"

"Oh, nothing." Lyn gave him a look. "It's just, if all you did was sit on the beach and read, why did you need two spoons for your ice cream?"

Aaron's mouth fell open as he scrambled to come up with a good answer. Lyn just grinned at him and swept out of the room, leaving him to stare after her.

Chapter Six

Lucky played the moment over and over until he fell asleep. Why had Aaron thrown him out after their date?

Of the two possibilities, Lucky wasn't sure which one he cared for less, since neither of them painted Aaron in a great light. It was possible that Aaron didn't want him to meet his family because of Lucky's skin color. Some parents didn't want their kids "associating" with him, simply because his father was white and his mother was Black. He hoped that wasn't it, but he couldn't discount it. Aaron's family seemed to be "old" money, if the size of their "house" was anything to go by. So race was a possibility. The other option was that Aaron was firmly in the closet, terrified his family would find out he was gay. Lucky could sympathize with that, of course.

He wasn't sure he could put up with either option, though. For days after the date, Lucky turned things over, hoping for a third option: that Aaron was just painfully shy, or something, anything.

Regardless of Aaron's reason for asking Lucky to leave, Lucky was sure of one thing: He wouldn't be anyone's dirty little secret. The fact that Aaron hadn't tried to contact him since that night wasn't helping his feelings.

He supposed the phone worked both ways, but Lucky hesitated every time he began to dial Aaron's number. If he asked Aaron outright what was going on, could he handle the answer? Did he even want to know?

It took him a week to decide that, if Aaron was still interested, he ought to let Aaron explain. Lucky sighed. Aaron still hadn't tried to contact him, so his week of agonizing might have all been for nothing. Maybe Aaron just didn't want to see him again. It would be upsetting; Lucky really, really liked Aaron and he wasn't sure he wanted their time together to be over so soon. He'd never had a connection with another guy so quickly, never had one spark his creativity at first glance the way Aaron had. Lucky didn't want let that go if he didn't have to.

He was glad it was his day off and that he had all day to stew about it in peace. His roommates were elsewhere, as usual. He picked up his phone and typed out a message. He hit send and then let out the breath he'd been holding.

It was up to Aaron now.

* * *

Aaron had spent most of the week wishing Lucky would text him, wondering how Lucky felt about the way their date ended, and feeling guilty about sneaking around. He hated his parents for putting him and Lyn in this position, he hated Lyn for pushing him toward Lucky, and he hated Lucky for not texting him.

He hated himself most of all.

Aaron was probably expecting too much. Maybe Lucky had only wanted one thing from him—maybe he was supposed to be a "hump and dump," as their friends in school used to say. Maybe Lucky had figured he wasn't worth the effort since he'd pretty much thrown the man out on his ass when Lucky had tried to kiss him.

Throughout the week, he'd done his best to distract himself. Aaron had spent time on the beach with Lyn, ignoring her curious gazes and questioning looks—there was no point in telling her about Lucky now, given the lack of contact. He'd gone for morning runs to clear his head and once even went as far as caddying for his and Lyn's fathers—which he hated with a vengeance. Desperate times called for desperate measures.

The dreaded dinner with Richard arrived, and, while Aaron was looking for distraction, this was not one that he wanted. The less time spent with Richard Peterman, the better. Lyn didn't seem to have the same opinion. She fluttered around the day of the dinner, making sure everything was "just so." He was ready to hide somewhere, anywhere, just to get away from her.

Richard showed up, prompt of course.

"Richard, my boy!" Charles Ledbetter crowed as he led Richard into the living room where they were all sitting. "Right on time."

The words were a punch to his stomach, a pointed reminder that Aaron was the reason they were having this dinner. Richard grinned, a toothy wide white grin. Aaron fought to keep from glaring. Aaron held his breath while Richard made the rounds, greeting the rest of the parentals. He'd brought large bouquets of flowers for his mother, Lyn's mother, and Lyn. Lyn actually gasped, as if she'd never gotten flowers before.

Richard seemed to monopolize the conversation during dinner, and Aaron couldn't decide if he was upset or thankful. His father's ever watchful gaze wasn't on him for a change, but his father—and everyone else—was hanging on Richard's every word. He wasn't sure how much longer he could make himself be polite. He was so, so tired of faking it every day of his life.

Lyn's repeated elbowing wasn't helping.

Dinner finally came to a close, though Aaron hadn't managed a get a bite down. He wanted nothing more than to go up to his room, climb into bed, and pull the covers over his head. Instead, he was forced to make nice over slices of baked Alaska, his least favorite desert.

He stabbed his food forcefully, imagining it was Richard's face, with his too-white smile and his stupid hair. He couldn't take it. He was going to get up and excuse himself, pleading a stomachache or food poisoning or the flu. Anything to get him away from this farce of a dinner, with Richard the perfect society son.

He realized that everyone was rising from the table. It was over.

Richard was shown out by the parentals, leaving him and Lyn for cleanup duty.

"What's with you tonight?" Aaron asked Lyn as he dried the plate she'd just handed him. "You seem more Stepford than usual."

"I don't know what you're talking about," Lyn replied, scrubbing unnecessarily at another plate. "What about you? You were almost rude, just sitting there, glaring."

"I wasn't glaring."

"Could have fooled me," Lyn snapped, dropping the plate in the soapy water. "You know, it'd be nice if you stopped and thought about someone other than yourself." She snatched the towel out of his hands, dried her hands, and tossed the towel on the counter. Aaron could only stare at her with his mouth hanging open.

As she stalked out of the room, Aaron said the only thing that came to mind: "But you don't even like Richard Peterman!"

In an uneasy truce the next morning they decided to spend time on the beach. It wasn't long before they found their old rhythm, laughing and talking as if Lyn's odd behavior the night before had never happened. After a while, Aaron stared out over the ocean, trying not to think of a certain someone.

His phone vibrated against his leg and he jumped. Aaron glanced at Lyn, asleep next to him on her beach chair, strategically staged to get the best tan possible. The text notification was lit up over his background picture, one of him and Lyn taken right before the end of school. He bit his lip. It had to be Lucky. He couldn't think of anyone else who would text him—Lyn was with him and both sets of parents were in town for the afternoon, busy with social and business commitments.

Taking a deep breath, Aaron reminded himself not to get his hopes up. Closing his eyes, he pressed the text message icon. He counted to five and then forced his eyes open.

"Oh my God," he whispered, his face lighting up with a smile. Aaron let out a chuckle at Lucky's message. He was feeling a million emotions at once. Mostly, he was relieved that he hadn't blown it; Lucky still wanted to see him.

Aaron immediately started planning.

* * *

THE NEXT DAY COULDN'T COME fast enough. It was a Saturday, and Lucky had to work the late shift, for which he was very glad. That meant that he could meet Aaron with no problems. Aaron had said he would take care of the planning, since he was familiar with the island and Savannah as well. Lucky tied his sneakers and headed outside toward the parking lot by the pier, crowded as it was with tourists and carnival goers, where he was going to meet up with Aaron.

He was startled when Aaron, his auburn hair tousled from the wind, pulled up in front of him in a dark blue convertible. Aaron lifted his sunglasses and grinned up at Lucky.

"Need a ride, good sir?"

Lucky let out a surprised laugh. The difference between the Aaron in front of him and the one from the other night was drastic. He wasn't sure what could have brought about such a change, but he was going to enjoy it. He hopped into the car, not even bothering to open the door. Aaron stared at him, wide-eyed.

"Drive on, Jeeves," Lucky said once he fastened his seatbelt.

"Your wish is my command," Aaron replied as they left the parking lot. Lucky stared at the inspiring beauty of the coast as they headed into Savannah. He was so glad to have been able to leave Texas and see some of the country before school. He couldn't wait to get back to his room and draw some of the landscapes. Out of the corner of his eye,

Lucky watched Aaron drive. Aaron wouldn't tell him where they were going, but they were headed into Savannah and away from the island. It seemed as if Aaron had planned this so they wouldn't run into his family, but Lucky didn't consider that idea too long. He had promised himself that he would give Aaron another chance and suspecting him of that was not giving him a fair shot.

Aaron asked about his carnival job, and Lucky spent the rest of the drive filling Aaron in on his art teacher and what he liked and didn't like about the carnival. Aaron kept asking questions. He laughed at Lucky's impressions of the customers he'd had. Aaron's laugh was joyful and light, and Lucky committed to it memory. He wanted to draw the joy that Aaron was exuding.

Finally Aaron pulled into a parking lot and turned off the car. Lucky took in the scenery, but he wasn't sure what to look for, so it didn't help clear up the mystery.

"Come on," Aaron said, ushering him out of the car. Lucky let Aaron lead the way, walking until they were in front of a large white building with four columns in front.

"Welcome to the Telfair Art Museum," Aaron announced with an exaggerated wave of his hand. "The first public art museum in the south."

Lucky's mouth fell open. "What are we waiting for?" Lucky asked. "Let's go!"

Aaron paid the admission fee for both of them despite Lucky's protests; he led Lucky into the first exhibit and they began wandering around. Lucky was less familiar with some of the American painters on display, but he enjoyed the works immensely. He and Aaron walked from piece to piece, giving them all equal consideration. Lucky walked as close to Aaron as he dared, wondering what Aaron would do if Lucky took him by the hand. He didn't though. Instead, he got lost in the art, explaining to Aaron about the different techniques and styles the artists used. Aaron seemed content to let him talk even when it was clear he wasn't getting the same things from the art and he smiled when Lucky would go on and on about one of the works.

"Am I boring you?" Lucky asked. That was the last thing he wanted to do.

"No," Aaron said softly. "I think I could listen to you talk about art all day."

Lucky couldn't help but smile.

"You're sweet," he said. Aaron blushed.

"What's your favorite work of art?" Aaron asked as they made their way out of the museum and back to the car.

"*Starry Night* by Vincent van Gogh."

"I've actually seen that one. What do you like about it?"

"It's peaceful," Lucky replied. He pictured the painting, the swirls of light and color taking shape as he talked about them. "There's so much love in that painting. Sort of like the town is being taken care of by the light of the stars."

"Wow," Aaron said quietly. "I never considered it that way. I always feel like I'm as swirled inside as the painting when I see it."

Lucky looked at him for a long moment, so Aaron changed the subject by asking him what other artists he enjoyed. Lucky sat back in the seat, and talked about art while Aaron drove them back to the island.

It had been a truly wonderful day.

Aaron didn't want the day to end. He didn't want to part ways with Lucky, to go back to the beach house and deal with his family. Even going through the drive thru for snacks hadn't added enough time. He was enjoying being hidden from the world with nothing but Lucky to worry about. Lucky had to work though, so it was out of Aaron's hands.

He dropped Lucky at the carnival and smiled as they came to a stop.

"Thank you for coming with me," Aaron murmured.

"I had a great time," Lucky said. Aaron grinned, happy that his idea had panned out. Lucky gave him a long look, and there was a pregnant pause. Aaron wanted nothing more than to kiss Lucky and he was pretty sure Lucky wanted that to, but Aaron couldn't. Not here. Not with all these people around.

He gave Lucky another smile before turning to face the wheel. "We should do this again soon."

Lucky nodded, his expression indicating that he wasn't sure what to make of Aaron's behavior. "Sure."

Lucky got out of the car without another word and headed into the carnival. Aaron pulled away when Lucky was no longer visible in the crowd. He sighed and steered the car back toward the beach house.

Aaron's phone chimed as he put the car in park and turned it off. He smiled as he checked his phone; he had a text from Lucky.

A thrill shot through him—Lucky had obviously enjoyed their date if he wanted to see him again. Aaron bit his lip, wondering if he could find more time away from his responsibilities. His parents would probably buy him going out for a run along the beach, and Lyn wouldn't want to join him for that. He texted Lucky with a place to meet: a wooded area where they could be alone and away from prying eyes.

Chapter Seven

Lucky wandered close to the edge of the wooded area. He heard the waves crashing onto the beach in the distance. The air was cool but he didn't feel cold; his entire body thrummed with anticipation. Aaron was still interested in him. He had to tread carefully though; he didn't want another false start. His mother's warnings about boys only wanting one thing and then leaving chose that moment to pop into his head, and Lucky pushed them away. Aaron wasn't like that. He may not have known Aaron for very long, but he knew that much.

The sound of shoes scuffling in the dirt got his attention and Lucky looked up, smiling when he saw Aaron. Thanks to his time in the sun, Aaron's skin was pale gold in the moonlight. He was so beautiful it made Lucky ache.

"Hi," Aaron whispered.

"Hi," Lucky replied.

An awkward silence fell over them. Lucky searched desperately for something to say, but nothing came to mind. They'd seen each other just hours earlier, and it hadn't been like this, maybe because he'd been yammering about art nonstop or maybe because it wasn't dark and romantic and they hadn't been alone.

"Have you been in here before?" Aaron asked, gesturing to the woods behind them.

"No." Lucky shook his head. In his limited time off from the carnival, he'd not given the woods a lot of consideration as a place to spend his time.

"Come on," Aaron said, moving into the tree line. "There's this clearing. I think you're going to love it." They walked in silence for several moments. Aaron seemed to know exactly where he was going. Lucky took the opportunity to study Aaron as they walked; his fingers tingled. He wanted to draw this moment or paint it. Paint might be better.

"What?" Aaron asked, sounding self-conscious.

"You look beautiful in the moonlight. Your skin glows."

"Oh," Aaron mumbled, his face turning red. Lucky loved that Aaron blushed all the time. It endeared Aaron to him. "I don't know what to say. Thank you?"

"You're welcome." Lucky chuckled. He liked that he could make Aaron nervous. He liked knowing he affected Aaron.

"I was really glad when you texted me," Aaron said, his voice soft. "I'm glad you had a good time today."

"I did." Lucky took a deep breath. He had a few questions and he needed to know the answers, even if he didn't really want to hear them. "Can we talk about what happened after our first date?"

Aaron looked stricken, but Lucky pressed on.

"I wasn't upset, really," he told Aaron, who looked relieved. "Confused, at first. If you're not out to your family, though, it's not my place to judge. Everyone comes out at their own pace."

Aaron let out a shuddering breath. "Lyn's the only one who knows."

Lucky wanted to know everything, wanted to know why Aaron looked as though he was going to throw up or hyperventilate at the mere thought of his parents knowing he was gay.

"That sounds terrible," Lucky commented. Aaron shrugged, and Lucky figured he wouldn't press anymore. "My mother reacted by telling me that boys only want one thing."

Aaron stumbled over a tree branch and nearly went down. Lucky rushed to help him and Aaron's gaze met his. A charged moment passed between them, and Lucky barely dared to breathe. Aaron pulled away, looking more flustered than ever, so Lucky changed the subject.

"So, where exactly are you absconding to with me?"

"You'll see," Aaron replied with a mysterious smile, and the tension dissipated.

They broke through the last of the trees, entering a clearing. A section of sky was visible; the stars shone brightly overhead. There was a thick carpet of grass under their feet, and Lucky couldn't hear anything except the wind through the trees and the insects chirping around them.

He wanted to draw the scene. It was inspiring. His fingers actually twitched. How did this boy come to know him so well in such a short time?

"Aaron, it's amazing," Lucky told him. "You were right. I love it."

Aaron smiled from ear to ear. "I love it here, too," Aaron said, turning slowly in a circle and staring up at the trees and sky above them. "When I'm here, I feel like I'm nowhere. Nothing can touch me here. There are no expectations."

"Thank you for bringing me here." Lucky couldn't take his eyes off Aaron. Seeing his joy at sharing this place, the fact that Aaron had actually brought Lucky to a place that was so special to him, Lucky was moved. He stepped closer to Aaron as Aaron stopped his spin. They faced each other, gazes locked. Lucky's heart was pounding so hard, he feared it might burst right out of his chest. He had to kiss Aaron and he had to kiss him *right now*.

He moved even closer; his hand reached up to caress Aaron's cheek. He needed to know if Aaron's skin was as soft as it looked, and his brush against Aaron's nose hadn't answered that question. Aaron was breathing heavily, his eyes wide as he held Lucky's gaze. Lucky tilted his head, leaning forward.

Loud music made them jump. Aaron frantically dug into his pocket, pulled out his phone, and glared at the offending device. He glanced at the caller ID and groaned. Lucky sighed. Aaron talked rapidly with someone Lucky presumed was Lyn. The call ended after a second, and Aaron turned back to him.

"I have to go," Aaron said. "I don't want to but—"

"It's okay," Lucky told him. He wasn't going to make Aaron's home situation any more complicated than it needed to be.

"I'll walk you to the beach," Aaron offered. Lucky nodded and they made their way out of the woods.

Aaron didn't pause when they hit the tree line, just turned around to face Lucky, walking backward. "I'll text you later, I promise."

"You better," Lucky said before he could stop himself.

"I will."

Aaron turned around and jogged off, leaving Lucky alone in the darkness.

* * *

THE TEXT CONVERSATIONS WITH LUCKY were the only thing that got Aaron through the following week. His parents were planning a Fourth of July party, which would end with everyone walking to the pier to watch the fireworks. Aaron dreaded the entire event. It would be the same as every other party his parents had ever thrown: nothing but business talk and socialites as far as the eye could see. He tried telling Lyn as much, but she'd just said she was looking forward to it.

He didn't understand that; in the past she'd detested those events just as he had. They'd have to pretend for hours, forcing fake smiles while picking at ridiculous food and dodging questions about when they were getting married. She'd never had a positive thing to say about one of them. He'd tried talking to her about it, but their mothers had corralled her to do all the jobs that he wasn't assigned.

Talking to Lucky kept him sane. He wished they could see each other again, but between party prep and Lucky's work schedule, it just hadn't happened. He toyed with inviting Lucky to the party but he couldn't. His parents would probably freak out—a bi-racial carnival worker in their living room? And if they happened to find out Lucky was gay?

He shook his head. Aaron didn't even want to consider what would happen then. Besides, he'd have to spend the entire night with Lyn on his arm, and there was so much that Lucky didn't know, information and worries and *plans* he hadn't had the courage to share. There would be no way to hide the truth if Lucky was there.

He sighed, taking advantage of the first few minutes of peace he'd had all week. The mothers were at the spa again, getting beautified. His father was playing a round of golf with Mr. Peterman. That left Aaron home alone, much to his relief, waiting for the caterers and the decorators to arrive and start setting up.

His phone vibrated.

I miss you.

He quickly texted back that he missed Lucky too, and it was true. He wished he could find a way.

Aaron bit his lip; an idea popped into his head. At the end of the party, everyone would walk down the beach to watch the fireworks. Aaron was pretty sure that his parents wouldn't be able to keep track of him in the crowd. Maybe he could slip away.

Aaron sent Lucky another text.

Meet me at the woods tonight for the fireworks?

His phone vibrated again. Aaron took a deep breath and read Lucky's answer.

I thought you'd never ask.

Chapter Eight

Lucky couldn't wait for midnight. The carnival would be open later than usual due to the holiday, but luckily he'd had the earlier shift. That had given him time to stop by the trailer, shower and change for his date with Aaron, and then spend the rest of his time freaking out. He was starting to think that maybe there was a curse on his and Aaron's relationship. It shouldn't be nearly this hard for two teenage boys to lock lips.

It was driving him crazy; he couldn't stop imagining it. He had to know if Aaron's lips were as soft as they looked, how they would feel pressed against his. He moaned quietly, stopping that train of thought. Walter was working a late shift, but Bud was due back any second, and he did not have time to deal with anything those ideas might lead to. Instead, he decided to pack a bag. He reached under his bed and pulled out his duffel bag, then quickly shoved a blanket, bottled water, and his sketchpads into it. A flashlight followed. He bit his lip and checked his watch, sighing because not much time had passed.

His phone rang then, making him jump. Lucky answered it without looking. "Aaron?"

"No," his mother's voice sounded in his ear. He groaned silently.

"Mom, hi! How are you? How's Austin?"

"I'm tired," his mother answered. That was her standard answer every time they talked, and Lucky hated it. He hated more that he couldn't do anything about it. "Hot. Who's Aaron?"

"Mama," he protested. He didn't want to get into this with her. The last time he'd talked to her about Aaron, she'd been less than supportive.

"Jonas, we talked about this. This summer is for work experience and to further your career. Not for boys."

"Mama," Lucky cut her off. "Stop."

"Why do I even bother?" His mother sighed. "You never listen to me anyway. You'll come home with a broken heart, young man, and then where will you be? You mark my words."

"Noted. Look, I gotta go. I'll call you tomorrow, okay?"

"Jonas—"

"Bye, Mama, love you!"

He hung up the phone and sank onto his bed, feeling drained. He needed time to pass faster. He needed to get his mother's words out of his head. She was wrong.

She had to be.

Aaron had assumed it would be more difficult to get away from the party. He'd found Lyn in the crowd, and told her he wasn't feeling well and he was going back to the house and to bed. She said she'd cover for him. Their parents had stopped paying attention to their every move once the party had shifted to the pier to get ready for the fireworks. Still, Lyn just nodded, looking distractedly at her watch as he slipped away.

He headed quickly away from the pier. The beach was quiet once he was away from the crowd, and he sped up, anxious to see Lucky again. He'd focused on nothing else since the plans had been made. He was going to kiss Lucky tonight, even if it killed him. Nerves roiled his stomach, and he took some deep breaths, trying to keep calm. He couldn't kiss Lucky if he threw up or fainted—that would not go over well at all. Aaron paused and made sure his phone was on silent when he approached the tree line. He didn't want any interruptions.

"Lucky?" he called softly.

"Hey," Lucky's voice came from the shadows. Aaron closed his eyes in relief.

"Hi." Aaron grinned. He couldn't help feeling giddy. They didn't speak beyond that, and Aaron headed for the clearing while Lucky fell in behind him. He labored for something to say, something clever and witty, but he had nothing. He was terrible at this.

Soft skin brushed against his fingers, and then Lucky's hand slid into his. Aaron stifled his startled inhalation as he glanced at Lucky in the darkness. He was pretty sure Lucky was grinning, and Aaron grinned back. They made their way through the trees quickly and Aaron startled when Lucky pulled out a blanket to put on the ground.

Lucky sat and patted the space next to him. "Do you think we'll be able to see fireworks from here?"

Aaron sat, then looked at the tree tops. "If they're high enough, maybe." He bit his lip and meeting Lucky's gaze. "But if I'm being honest, that's not why I came out here."

"Me either," Lucky whispered, an intense look in his eyes. Aaron suddenly lost his ability to breathe. Lucky leaned forward, and Aaron couldn't tear his gaze from Lucky's mouth.

Aaron barely had time to take in another breath before Lucky's lips were touching his. Aaron froze. He didn't know what to do. Lucky's lips were insistent though, and Aaron's lips finally conveyed to his brain the information that he was being very seriously kissed. He instinctively kissed back ad Lucky's hands cradled his face.

Lucky broke the kiss, and Aaron stared at him, his breath coming in pants. "Wow."

The sounds of fireworks boomed in the distance, and flashes of light appeared overhead.

"Literal fireworks," Aaron whispered as they glanced upward. Lucky let out a laugh, and Aaron joined in. He'd just had his first real kiss and it had been absolutely mind-blowing.

“Stay just like that,” Lucky said, his laughter trailing off. Aaron did as he was told, watching out of the corner of his eye as Lucky moved the flashlight closer and picked up his pad of paper.

Aaron couldn’t think of a better way to spend the evening than staring at the night sky while Lucky drew him. He didn’t want it to end, but when the fireworks drew to a close forty-five minutes later he’d have to go. He told Lucky, and they reluctantly made their way back out to the beach.

“I wish...” Aaron began, trying to come up with words, even though none of them would come close to expressing what he was feeling. For some things, words were inadequate. This moment was one of them. He shook his head and then leaned up a little, kissing a surprised Lucky lightly on the mouth. Lucky’s arms went around his waist and Aaron’s hands gripped Lucky’s shoulders as the kiss deepened. Dear God, if this was what kissing was like, he was in so much trouble. He was never going to want to do anything else.

* * *

Aaron spent most of the next day carrying his father’s bag as he followed him and Ronald Rossman around the golf course. It was mentally exhausting, physically draining, and only made better due to the near-constant texts from Lucky.

Their conversation continued back and forth. Lucky mostly commented on the people at his booth or walking by. It was all Aaron could do to stifle his laughter and not fall behind. If his father noticed his lack of attention, he didn’t say anything. Aaron was pretty sure he’d gotten away with it when they arrived home and he was dismissed to go find Lyn on the beach.

Aaron wasted no time shucking his golfing clothes for a bathing suit. He made his way to the beach and found Lyn camped out under their bright beach umbrella, Kindle in hand.

"Reading anything good?" he asked, settling on the blanket beside her.

"Oh, not really." Lyn set down her Kindle. He tried to see what she was reading and only caught a glimpse of the text; the word "ship" was all that registered before the screen went dark. "How was golf?"

"Excruciating." Aaron moaned, leaning back so he could stretch out, digging his toes in the sand. His feet were killing him, and the rough sand was wonderful under his toes. Aaron's phone vibrated and he smiled as he read through the text Lucky had just sent him.

"Who is that from?" Lyn asked with a raised eyebrow.

"No one." Aaron looked away from her to stare out at the ocean. He wasn't used to keeping secrets from Lyn. She'd been his best friend practically since birth, and he'd never kept anything from her.

"Aaron..." she trailed off, sounding uncertain. "You can tell me anything, you know that, right?"

He shrugged; he'd never imagined that there would be something he couldn't—*wouldn't*—tell her. He had never considered that he would want to have something that was just his, something that was untainted by the rest of his life.

Being with Lucky was liberating in a way that Aaron hadn't known existed, and he couldn't take the chance of anything or anyone ruining it. Even his best friend.

They fell into an uneasy silence then, the quiet somehow louder than the crashing waves and noise of the other beachgoers around them. With a sigh Lyn turned on her Kindle when it was clear he wasn't going to say anything further. Aaron turned his gaze to the water, losing himself in thoughts of Lucky.

It was almost a relief when they had to pack up and go inside for dinner, even though the conversation was dominated by business. Aaron hadn't realized how much their fathers discussed it until now. If he never heard another word about Ledbetter, Inc., it would be too soon.

He complimented his mother on dinner as soon as he could and thankfully she prattled on about the local vegetables she'd gotten her hands on for the salad.

He held in his sigh and was glad when he could escape upstairs.

Lucky was pretty sure he was going to replay that kiss over and over for the rest of his life: the feel of Aaron's lips against his, the smell of his skin, the touch of his fingers as they dug into Lucky's shoulders. The moment had been magical, something Lucky had been dreaming about since he'd seen his first Disney movie and had fallen in love with the idea of falling love.

He wanted to shout it from the rooftops, to brag about it to someone, scream it to anyone who would listen. There was no one to tell, though–his mother wouldn't want to hear about it and his roommates, well that wasn't going to happen. He could have texted friends from high school, but ultimately hadn't. He wasn't sure they'd want to hear the details, no matter how cool they'd been about his sexuality back in school. So he went to bed, pulled up the covers, and relived that moment until he fell asleep.

He woke up happy and with tons of energy, and texting Aaron between customers was the highlight of his day. He wanted to see Aaron again, but Aaron had been dragged off for some family thing and, once he was back in his trailer, Lucky had resigned himself to finishing the drawing of Aaron he'd started last night.

It wasn't perfect, no matter how much he tweaked it, but he loved the look on Aaron's face, the glow of the flashlight, and the fireworks captured in the shadows on the paper.

Bud entered the trailer and Lucky flipped his sketchpad shut, trying not to make it look as though he'd done it just because Bud was in the room. Bud barely gave him a glance though, but headed straight for his bed and turned on his little TV. Lucky sighed, taking a chance and flipping the sketchpad back open. He was just drawing. What would Bud care? He hadn't cared when Lucky had said he was gay.

"You got some talent," Bud's voice made him look up, and Lucky raised his head to see Bud staring at his sketchpad.

"Thanks," Lucky replied, trying not to show his surprise.

"That your fella?"

"Yeah."

Bud nodded and went back to his TV, and Lucky let out a breath he hadn't known he was holding.

He felt bad for misjudging Bud. Obviously, if the man was going to have an issue with Lucky's sexuality, he would have had it by now. Lucky resolved to make it up to him somehow.

Chapter Nine

AARON PICKED AT HIS PLATE, wishing dinner would just be over so he could go meet Lucky. His mind raced, trying to think up an excuse that would get him out of the house without Lyn. It wasn't that he couldn't go out without her, but their parents always encouraged them to spend time together. Normally, he wouldn't have minded; hanging out with his best friend was not a hardship—until now, when he needed to sneak away alone to seek Lucky.

His mother and Lyn's were clearing the table together when Aaron made his move. "I think I'm going to go for a jog," he blurted.

"You've been doing that a lot lately," his mother pointed out, but Aaron couldn't tell if she suspected something was going on or if she was just commenting on his recent behavior.

"It's nice," Aaron said, hoping they couldn't read any guilt on his face. He'd never lied to his parents so much in his life. "The beach is pretty empty, and, you know, exercise is healthy." Aaron winced. He couldn't believe those words had just come out of his mouth; that was the lamest excuse he'd ever heard. Lyn shot him a questioning glance, which he observed out of the corner of his eye. He didn't look at her. She was already aware that something was up, and he didn't want her to invite herself along. This thing between him and Lucky, whatever it was, he wanted to keep it between him and Lucky as long as he could.

When it was over, because it would have to end, right? He was too much of a realist to think otherwise. He'd need her then.

He refused to follow that line of thinking and stood up before anyone else could comment.

"I won't be long."

LUCKY HAD TO DRAW HIM again. It was like a sickness, this need to catch Aaron on paper. The clearing in the woods was becoming their place to meet, and Lucky couldn't be happier. He loved seeing Aaron, and his sketchbook was quickly filling up with Aaron in different poses. Lucky loved to experiment with the shadows and light that drawing in the dark afforded him.

He loved spending time with Aaron. Lucky had to stop himself from just staring at Aaron while they sat and talked. He loved the sound of Aaron's voice and the way he spoke about things. They could talk about anything it seemed–politics, musicals, art. The awkwardness from their first few meetings was gone. The only topic that seemed off limits was Aaron's family, and Lucky didn't want to push, not after the way Aaron had quickly changed the subject, but Lucky had to admit he was insanely curious.

When they fell silent, Lucky asked, "What's your family like?"

"They're... conservative," Aaron said after a long moment.

Lucky kept drawing, thinking of his mother. She didn't get him, not really. "I know what that's like."

"They mean well, I suppose."

"Yeah," Lucky agreed. "What about Lyn?"

"Oh," Aaron replied. Lucky could have sworn Aaron was nervous. "We've just known each other forever. She's my best friend."

"Does she know you come out here and meet me?"

Aaron shook his head. "But I'll tell her eventually." He stared at Lucky, and Lucky's heart did a somersault. "I wanted something that was just mine, for once. Something just for me, you know?"

"Yeah," Lucky said He understood that. Lucky dropped his sketchpad and charcoal stick on the blanket, moved toward Aaron, and sat up on his knees. He cupped his hands around Aaron's face, and his finger's caressed Aaron's skin gently. "I'm going to kiss you now," Lucky murmured. He had to, after what Aaron had said.

"Okay." Aaron's breath touched Lucky's lips, their faces were so close together. Lucky bridged the small gap; his lips touched Aaron's softly. He couldn't get enough of Aaron's mouth, of the way that Aaron would sink into their kisses, as if he'd never felt anything like them. It was a heady feeling, one that Lucky wanted to get lost in over and over. Aaron's hands went to Lucky's waist, and Lucky moved his hands up into Aaron's hair. He wanted more. He wanted this to never end.

"Lucky," Aaron panted as Lucky moved his lips along Aaron's jaw and down toward his neck. "*Oh.*" Aaron let out a moan and Lucky smiled against his neck. "Are–are..." Lucky loved the effect he was having on Aaron. He'd never rendered a guy speechless. "Are you—are we boyfriends?" Aaron finally managed to get out.

Lucky pulled back, looking into Aaron's eyes. "I'd like to be, if you want."

"Yes," Aaron whispered.

He wasn't sure who moved first, but they were kissing again. Lucky lost all rational thought. Aaron was his boyfriend. He had a *boyfriend*, his first real one. He didn't know if he'd pushed Aaron to the ground or if Aaron had pulled him down, but there they were, kissing as if the world was going to end. Lucky had had no idea it could be like this. He'd dreamed it, sure, but years of his mother's lectures had led him to think he'd been expecting too much.

Until Aaron, until now.

Tugging at Aaron's shirt, his hands moved from Aaron's hair down his chest to his waist. He needed more.

A loud beeping rang out in the clearing, and Aaron was suddenly gone from his arms, stumbling backward.

Aaron was panting; his clothes were as wild and as rumpled as Lucky's felt. Lucky wanted nothing more than to keep kissing him, to get lost in Aaron at the expense of the rest of the world. He didn't though, because he knew what words were coming next. The same words that had ended almost every other date they'd had.

"I have to go."

Lucky just nodded, watching as Aaron scrambled off into the trees. He took a deep breath and let it out slowly.

Even though it had ended abruptly, *again*, Lucky smiled as he looked up at the night sky.

He had a boyfriend.

* * *

AARON STUMBLED OUT OF BED the next morning, not caring how he looked. He'd come back from his "jog" to find most everyone in bed and Lyn nowhere to be seen. He'd been way more focused on Lucky and the fact that Lucky was his boyfriend now to pay much attention to her whereabouts. She knew just as well as he what was expected. The parentals would be all over her if she put even a toe out of line.

Thinking about Lucky put a smile on his face and drew his focus from Lyn's recent behavior. *He had a boyfriend.* Aaron wanted to shout it from the rooftops, wanted everyone to feel this joy he was feeling. He couldn't though. Keeping his feelings for Lucky inside caused an actual physical ache. He'd had no idea that one person could feel so many things at once. He didn't bother to shower or get dressed before going downstairs. The parentals would probably be out for the day at some activity or other, leaving him and Lyn to fend for themselves for breakfast. He loved those days, when he didn't have to start faking when the sun was barely up in the sky.

"Look what the cat dragged in," Lyn teased as he walked into the kitchen. Her long hair was pulled back into a ponytail, and her colorful sundress was perfect for the already warm morning. Aaron made a face at her and headed for the cabinet and his favorite box of cereal. He joined Lyn at the table, where she was delicately biting into a piece of grapefruit. "Seriously, did you even get any sleep last night?"

"Of course." Aaron shoved a bite of cereal into his mouth so he had an excuse not to say anything else.

"What is that?" Lyn asked after a quiet moment, pointing a finger at his neck.

"What's what?" Aaron put his hand up to his neck. Had Lucky accidentally given him hickey? Things had gotten rather heated the night before. How the hell would he explain this?

"This," Lyn said, licking her finger and then swiping it along Aaron's neck. "It looks like dirt or dust."

Aaron was transported back to the night before, to the moment when Lucky had kissed him senseless and run his charcoal-covered fingers through Aaron's hair.

"I don't know." Aaron feigned indifference. "I guess I must have brushed up against something while jogging last night."

"On the *beach*?" Her tone was disbelieving. Aaron shrugged, shoving a large bite of the crunchy cereal into his mouth to keep from answering. "What's up with that, anyway?" Lyn asked, cutting another triangle of her grapefruit neatly with her spoon. "You never jog. In fact, I'm pretty sure you studiously avoid all forms of exercise."

"It gets me out of the house," Aaron told her, hoping that partial honesty would get Lyn to stop asking questions. He didn't like keeping things from her, and she was making it difficult to keep doing so. Part of him wanted to spill all the details about him and Lucky, but he wasn't ready yet. "You're one to talk, tattoo girl."

Lyn looked at him before turning back to her grapefruit. He sensed he had gotten through this round, but the subject was not over with. He forced himself to finish his food; guilt churned his stomach and killed his appetite. He was lying to Lyn, the one person whom he'd never lied to, the one person who knew him better than everyone else in the world. Yet, as much as he hated it, he knew he was going to keep doing it.

He needed just a little more time.

Chapter Ten

"When did you know you were gay?"

Lucky looked up from his drawing, meeting Aaron's inquisitive gaze. He smiled and set down his pencil.

"I think I probably always knew," Lucky replied, "but the first time I *knew* I was fourteen." He leaned back on his free hand, looking up at the afternoon sky. They'd managed to get away during the day, something that Lucky was enjoying immensely. "I was looking at art online," he continued, "and I stumbled on a website I was way too young to be on." He laughed. "There was this sketch, this man… his pose was just breathtaking and he wasn't wearing a stitch of clothing." He glanced at Aaron, enjoying his boyfriend's red cheeks and wide eyes. "That's when I knew."

"Wow," Aaron exhaled, looking a shell-shocked. He had clearly not expected an answer like that, but Lucky wasn't embarrassed. He'd drawn the human form over and over for years now. Nudity in art was way too common to be embarrassing.

"What about you?" Lucky wanted to know about Aaron, too. He wanted to know more than what Aaron had told him—he wanted to get past Aaron's layers and find the man within. Aaron seemed startled and then averted his eyes. Lucky waited. He didn't want to push Aaron too hard. Accepting one's sexuality was different for everyone, and he didn't want to hit a nerve and ruin their time together.

"I kissed Lyn when I was thirteen," Aaron finally said in a rush. "She was my best friend, my… everything. I love her like no one else." He sighed. "And kissing her was like kissing my sister."

Lucky chuckled. "And kissing me?" he asked with an arched eyebrow. Aaron blushed even harder, if that was possible.

"Electric," Aaron mumbled, staring at his hands. Lucky moved closer, taking Aaron's hands in his own.

"Hey," Lucky said quietly. "You don't have to be embarrassed."

"I'm not used to feeling… like *this.*"

Lucky put his hand under Aaron's chin and raised Aaron's head so he could stare into Aaron's beautiful eyes. He wanted to paint them.

"It's the same for me," Lucky admitted. Aaron's lips found his before the words had finished leaving his mouth, but Lucky really didn't care.

"I never thought," Aaron murmured against his lips, "not a million years…"

"What?" Lucky managed to get out, between breath-stealing kisses.

"Just… *you.*" Aaron groaned into his mouth. "You make me crazy."

"Do I?" Lucky grinned as he angled his mouth along Aaron's jaw, heading for Aaron's neck. He loved every reaction that Aaron had to his touch; knowing that he could make someone else feel that good was the best feeling.

"Yes," Aaron sighed, his fingers tangling in Lucky's hair, the thick locks twining around Aaron's fingers. "If anyone had told me I was going to meet you…" he trailed off, but Lucky was busy, focused on tasting every inch of Aaron's collarbone with his tongue. Aaron kept making mewling noises, and Lucky felt proud. He had reduced Aaron to this. Aaron, who was so put together and straight-laced. Aaron, who, Lucky was pretty sure, had never done anything like this in his whole entire life.

It was a feeling that went right to Lucky's groin. He needed to touch, needed something more. He needed to take Aaron apart and put him back together. Lucky's hands went for Aaron's waist, tugged at Aaron's shirt, pulled it from where it was tucked into Aaron's shorts. One hand pushed the fabric up, and Lucky moaned a little, finding Aaron's lips with his own. Aaron's skin was incredible under his fingertips, smooth but firm. What he wouldn't give to see Aaron fully, to draw him like that sketch that had captured him so utterly at fourteen! That idea very nearly made him explode with pleasure, and it was only Aaron's voice that held him back.

"Lucky," Aaron exhaled, pulling away a little. "Can we… slow down?" He asked the question hesitantly, as if he assumed Lucky might say no.

Lucky blinked at Aaron, processing. Then he slowly pulled his hand away from Aaron's stomach, until it had left the confines of Aaron's shirt. "Yeah," he mumbled, trying to get his brain to process properly, a feat easier said than done with Aaron right there, looking extremely mussed.

"It's not that I didn't love it," Aaron hurriedly added, nearly tripping over his tongue to get the words out. "I did, I just…I've never… and I don't know…"

"Aaron," Lucky said, chuckling at Aaron's obvious awkwardness. "It's okay. Me neither. At least, not everything."

"Oh." Aaron sighed. "*Oh*. I thought… art, models…" He trailed off, obviously embarrassed.

"No," Lucky said with a small smile. "I may have seen my fair share of naked models, but drawing someone can be a pretty clinical experience. And I'm usually in class, surrounded by twenty other people."

"So you're not super crazy experienced?"

"Nope. Is that bad?"

"No!" The exclamation was quite forceful; another blush stained Aaron's cheeks.

"Look, it doesn't matter to me what we do or don't do." He sank back onto the ground and pulled Aaron down, wrapping Aaron in his arms. "All that matters is that we're together."

"You're amazing," Aaron told him softly after a moment's silence.

"Yeah," Lucky drawled in playful agreement, earning a chuckle and a light slap on the shoulder from Aaron. Lucky retaliated by drawing him in for another toe-curling kiss.

* * *

A FEW DAYS HAD PASSED since his last date with Lucky in the woods, and Aaron couldn't wait to see him again. They had tentative plans to meet that afternoon, and he was going to do whatever he could to make it happen.

Aaron didn't have a plan to get away yet, but he figured one would come to him over breakfast. He wasn't expecting a thick envelope with a Harvard logo on it to be sitting next to his plate of bacon and eggs. Lyn was sitting across from his empty seat, eating her own breakfast. She looked up, but he couldn't take his eyes away from the envelope.

"How?" he started to ask.

"It was messengered over this morning." Lyn answered his unfinished question. "When the housekeeper found it in the mailbox, your dad had her send it down."

Aaron should have known the good things wouldn't last. Once again, reality was slapping him in the face. His hands trembled as he opened the envelope. He ignored his food entirely. He wouldn't be eating it; there was no way he would be able to keep any of it down.

He pulled out the sheaf of papers and flipped through them. Here it was, his entire future. Aaron took a deep breath and skimmed the welcome letter, before flipping through the other pages. He now had his dorm information, his roommate assignment, and the requirements for his business major.

Aaron groaned, looking at the list. Nothing but business, math, and a few electives for the next four years of his life.

Lyn took the papers and murmured as she read over them.

"Intro to Business," she said. "That sounds interesting."

Aaron shrugged.

"Oh, and you get to take econ and stats your first semester."

"I had no idea you were so into math," Aaron replied, surprised. He didn't recall her gushing about math-related things when they were in high school. Lyn shrugged, handed the papers back to him, and speared a piece of scrambled egg with her fork. He put the papers back in the envelope, clenching it tightly in his fist as he got up from the table.

He needed some air.

Aaron should have known that Lucky was going to question things he would rather he wouldn't—he just didn't understand why it had to be today of all days, when he was already reeling from getting his Harvard packet. It was bound to happen, he figured; He was keeping things from Lucky; he was keeping Lucky from his family; and something had to give, right? But why did it have to be the same day?

It started innocently enough. Lucky was drawing, as usual. They'd gone to the pier this time. Aaron sneaked off while his father was in town and his mother was off with Lyn's mother and Lyn was… he didn't even know. Before Aaron met Lucky, he would have known every moment of Lyn's day, right down to the food she planned to eat. Hell, he'd have been there with her for most, if not all, of it. Now he couldn't remember the last time he'd spent any significant time with her. Aaron sighed. He hoped Lyn could forgive him being a crappy friend.

"Everything okay?" Lucky asked, staring off into the distance at a bird swooping toward the ocean waves. His pencil moved rapidly across the paper, trying to get the image down.

"I'm fine," Aaron replied, hating himself. He wasn't fine. He was the farthest thing from fine. He was a liar, and one of these days the guilt was going to get to him and he would crack; he would explode from the strain of keeping his feelings bottled up. He didn't know how to do it anymore. He'd gotten in so deep, too deep. He couldn't imagine his life without Lucky in it now, and that was a problem. And he had no one to talk to about any of it.

"So what made you choose Harvard?" Lucky asked.

"Hmmm?"

"Harvard," Lucky repeated gently. He touched Aaron's hand, and Aaron jumped, pulling away as though he'd come into contact with a live wire. *What if someone had seen?* "Seriously, what's with you?" Lucky asked, sounding both upset and concerned. "You've been weird the entire time we've been out here."

"I'm sorry, I..." Aaron trailed off. He didn't know what to say. *My family has no idea I'm gay. I'm going to marry Lyn someday. This can't ever be anything because you're a wonderful man who should never be second to anyone.* "I don't feel well," Aaron forced the words out. "I think I'm going to head home."

"I'll walk you," Lucky offered, but Aaron shook his head; his stomach and mind were churning. He couldn't do this anymore. He didn't say anything else, just turned and headed up the beach toward the house.

WITH A SINKING FEELING IN his stomach, Lucky watched Aaron go. He couldn't help but hear his mother's voice: "I told you so" resounding over the noise of the crashing waves and the carnival din. He sighed.

He tried to put Aaron out of his mind as he headed into the carnival and to his booth. He had a long shift ahead of him. By now it was routine: kids requesting to be drawn as superheroes or ponies, and just now a guy wanting to be drawn as an elf.

As elf guy took his picture and left, blonde hair and delicate skin gleaming in the sunlight behind one of the carnival trailers caught his attention and Lucky blinked. If he wasn't mistaken, it was Lyn. Lyn, who looked as if she was getting up close and personal with a guy who would not be out of place in an Abercrombie and Fitch catalog. He shouldn't have kept staring, but he was startled. Despite the limited time he'd spent with her, Lyn didn't strike him as the make-out-in-public type.

Almost as if she could sense him looking, their gazes suddenly locked. She was surprised, then horrified, and, the next thing he knew, she'd pulled the guy out of sight. Lucky shrugged. It wasn't any of his business what she did, even if her behavior did seem a little odd. He turned back to his booth. His next customer was a little boy who wanted to be drawn flying on a broomstick. Lucky went back to concentrating on his work.

He couldn't keep Aaron far from his thoughts, though. He nearly texted Aaron twenty times before finally turning off his phone. Lucky ran his hands through his hair, not caring that it was probably sticking up way more than usual as a result.

After work he wanted to crawl into bed and never get out, and yet he couldn't help the small part of him that wished he was meeting Aaron later.

He didn't expect find Aaron sitting on the steps of his trailer, looking sheepish.

AARON HAD INTENDED TO GO home after leaving Lucky. He'd meant to find Lyn, hang out on the beach, and try to relax. He couldn't, though. He'd started back to the beach house but found he couldn't face the possibility of running into his family. And, he was tired of lying to Lyn. He still hadn't figured out how to tell her the truth, but for now that was secondary. He also couldn't let things between him and Lucky stay the way they were.

So he had ended up here, sitting on Lucky's front stoop and feeling like an idiot. He hadn't meant to end up at Lucky's. He'd started walking and found himself in the trailer area behind the carnival. He'd asked a passing worker which one Lucky was staying in and then settled himself to wait.

Aaron was sure his emotions were written all over his face, especially when Lucky came around the corner and stopped upon seeing him.

"Hi," Aaron said softly.

"Hi."

"I couldn't leave things like that," Aaron said before Lucky could say anything else. "I just…"

"You don't have to tell me anything you don't want to. I shouldn't have pushed."

"No, you didn't," Aaron replied. "It's me, it's my issues," he tried to explain.

"Aaron, it's fine." Lucky moved passed him, put the key in the handle of the trailer, and unlocked the door.

"It's not *fine*!" Aaron burst out, his voice cracking hard with emotion. A few tears spilled onto his cheeks before he could force them back. He'd been repressing his real feelings about everything for years, and now he found he couldn't. Lucky eyed him with surprise written on his face.

"Come inside," Lucky offered, holding the door open.

Aaron nodded, sniffling and following Lucky into the trailer. He was startled by the sparse furnishings: three beds, limited storage space, and a door he assumed was to the bathroom.

"You have roommates?" Aaron asked, suddenly feeling nervous. He couldn't do this, not where people could see.

"Yeah. They won't be back 'til later, though."

Aaron bit his lip. Lucky sat on the edge of one of the beds, and Aaron assumed it was his own. He thought about sitting next to Lucky, but he wasn't sure he could get the words out and tell Lucky what he needed to tell him if he was sitting next to him.

"My family is complicated," Aaron finally began. "And there's a lot of… expectations. My whole life, I've been… lacking, at least in my father's eyes." He paused, trying to explain in a way that didn't reveal his family's expectations where Lyn was concerned. "I feel like nothing I do is good enough." Aaron's throat tightened, and it was a struggle to get the words out. "Do you know what it's like to go through every day and not know if your parents really love you? Or if what you've done that day is enough to earn it?"

"No, I don't," Lucky said softly, his eyes full of compassion. Aaron almost turned away; his feelings threatened to overwhelm him.

"And then I hit my teen years and I figured out that I like boys," Aaron forced himself to continue. He'd never talked with anyone about this, not this way. Not even Lyn. "God, I'm already not good enough for my parents and then I'm gay on top of it. Can you imagine?"

Lucky looked pained, and Aaron took a heaving breath. His perfectly maintained facade was gone, and the scared, confused boy that he really was had emerged.

"I don't want to go to Harvard," Aaron admitted in a choked voice, before Lucky could reply. Weirdly, saying the words out loud made him feel a little bit lighter. He'd actually said the words to someone. He knew he should tell Lucky about all of it, about his family's expectations for him and Lyn, but this was enough for today. "And I can't *not* go." Aaron let out a slightly hysterical sounding laugh. "That's not an option."

"Why not?"

Lucky wouldn't understand; Lucky had lived an independent life, one with no forced expectations. He would never be able to comprehend the kind of pressure that Aaron was under. Aaron laughed again, harsher this time, sinking down on the bed next to Lucky.

"What do *you* want to do?" Lucky said. He couldn't possibly know it, but that might have been the best thing he could have said. It made Aaron's swirling mass of emotions pause while he stared at his boyfriend. Tears welled up in his eyes again.

"I don't think anyone's ever bothered to ask me that." Even his teachers and classmates had assumed he'd be taking over the family business and had steered him toward all things boat- and business-related.

"I'm asking." Lucky's fingers brushed Aaron's cheek, wiping a tear that had managed to fall.

"I have absolutely no idea." Aaron loved the feel of Lucky's fingers against his skin. His eyes met Lucky's, and he was nearly bowled over by the intensity in Lucky's gaze. Any thought of this thing with Lucky just being a fling dissipated in that moment. Aaron had been fooling himself all along. There was no way this wasn't going to end messily and break both of their hearts. He never should have started it.

He couldn't bring himself to regret it, though. He'd spend the rest of his life broken-hearted if he could engrave the memory of this moment.

"I want *you*." The words slipped out of Aaron's mouth in a whisper before he could stop them. It was the only thing he knew to be true.

Lucky inhaled sharply, and Aaron closed his eyes in embarrassment. He wanted to take those words back.

Lucky's lips pressed against his softly, and Aaron's eyes shot open in surprise before shutting again. He fell deeper under Lucky's spell, barely noticing when Lucky pushed him onto his back on the bed. Lucky hovered over him, kissing him senseless. Nothing else mattered to him but Lucky and this moment. He tugged at Lucky's shirt, needing to get at Lucky's skin. Lucky pulled back just long enough to help Aaron slip the shirt over his head and toss it to the floor. Aaron wasted no time putting his hands on Lucky, enjoying the feel of Lucky's chest. Lucky was firm but not built: completely perfect.

The only sounds were their heavy breaths and their lips smacking lightly as they kissed. Lucky's fingers went to work on the buttons on Aaron's shirt and Aaron took that opportunity to explore Lucky's neck with his lips, teeth, and tongue. The taste of Lucky's skin was intoxicating, and the feel of Lucky's barely there stubble vibrating across his lips was almost too much to handle. The feel of the cool air in the trailer spread across his chest; Lucky had somehow unbuttoned his shirt without him realizing it. It was mind-boggling—he'd worn much less on the beach just the other day, and yet Aaron felt more naked in this moment, under Lucky's piercing gaze.

A loud banging startled them and Lucky practically jumped off him, leaving Aaron panting on the bed, his eyes wide. "Bud!" Lucky exclaimed, sounding embarrassed. "I thought you weren't coming back until later."

"Finished early," Bud said. Aaron went to work on the buttons of his shirt, feeling far too exposed. "Didn't mean to interrupt."

"You didn't," Lucky said, still sounding odd. "We were just…"

"I can see what you were just," Bud muttered, averting his gaze. "I got eyes."

"I should go," Aaron managed to get out, standing up. He wanted nothing more than to leave this room; mortification and panic swirled inside him. He'd been so stupid, coming here. Nothing Lucky had said had changed anything and now *someone knew…*

He frantically fixed his clothing and practically stumbled out the door in his haste. Lucky followed him outside, seeming at a loss for words.

"That was…" Aaron trailed off, not knowing what to say. The urge to flee was front and center; he had to get out of there.

"Awkward," Lucky offered, finding his voice. Aaron nodded. The whole day had been one series of emotions after another, and he wasn't sure how to put his mind around any of it. There was only one thing that was a fact: he cared too much about Lucky to let him go.

"I'll call you," Aaron said. He put his hands on Lucky's waist and pulled him close. He'd made this decision; he'd fallen for Lucky and he was going to see where it led him, even if it killed him in the process.

Lucky was still bare chested; his shirt was forgotten on the trailer floor. Aaron kissed him softly, trying to convey everything he was feeling in the press of his lips. He wasn't sure if he succeeded but they were both breathing heavily.

"I'll be waiting," Lucky said as they broke apart. It took a lot for Aaron to pull himself away from Lucky but he managed it, knowing he had to get home. He had no idea what he would tell his family about his whereabouts, but he didn't care. He could still feel Lucky's lips pressed against his, the smell of Lucky's skin still danced under his nose, and the sound of Lucky's panting still whispered in his ears.

Nothing else mattered.

Nothing.

When Lucky went back into the trailer, he had no idea what to expect. Knowing Lucky was gay and actually see it were two different things, and he had no idea what Bud would do. He'd worried for nothing though, because Bud was tucked up in bed, sound asleep. He must have wanted a nap after his shift. Lucky stared at him and then sighed and headed out to grab some food; maybe things would start making some kind of sense with a full stomach.

He focused on Aaron during his short walk into town. Aaron's emotional outburst earlier this afternoon made so much more sense now that he knew Aaron was upset about having to go to Harvard. Lucky had unintentionally struck a nerve and pushed Aaron too far.

Why Aaron didn't just tell his parents to shove it and do what he wanted, Lucky had no idea, but clearly not all families were like Lucky's. His mother had been strict but fair, letting him explore everything about art. She'd worked far too many hours in order to put him in the best classes, and he would be forever thankful. He might not agree with everything she said—she was wrong about men and she was wrong about Aaron—but she'd supported his dreams. He'd forgotten that not everyone had a mother like his.

He let himself into the restaurant; the smells of food cooking washed over him, making his stomach rumble. He immediately focused on what he was going to order. Lucky didn't realize he wasn't paying attention to where he was going until he bumped into someone.

"I am so sorry!" Lucky exclaimed, reaching out automatically to steady the person he'd nearly knocked over. "Lyn!"

"Lucky, hi!" Lyn greeted, looking flustered. "What are you doing here?"

"Getting some dinner."

"Right, yeah, food," she said, letting out a breath. "Cause it's a restaurant."

"So it is."

Where had the playful teasing girl he'd met before gone? Lyn looked panicked, clutching her food bag so tightly in her hands her knuckles were turning white.

"Everything okay?" he asked.

"Fine! You?"

"Great."

"Great!" Lyn smiled brightly. "I should go."

"Oh, yeah, don't let me keep you," Lucky said as Lyn moved past him, heading for the door.

She walked swiftly to a dark-colored SUV in the parking lot and hopped in. The SUV took off. An unfamiliar guy was driving the car; he was unsure if it was that guy he'd seen her with earlier in the day. He shook his head as he placed his order, then sat in the corner away from the other patrons. He didn't want to be around anyone right now. He wanted to remember how Aaron had been, so willing and responsive. He would remember the sounds that Aaron had made for the rest of his life and, he hoped, relive them every night in his dreams.

Lucky finished his food quickly; the hamburger and fries satisfied his hunger nicely. His phone buzzed and he checked it, seeing a text from Aaron.

Thinking about you.

Lucky wasted no time texting back.

Same here.

He couldn't help the smile that crossed his face. He had it bad for Aaron. Really bad.

Thank you for talking to me tonight.

Lucky sent the text and then cleared his trash. His phone buzzed again on his way out of the restaurant.

Thank you for listening.

Lucky made his way back to his trailer. Walter would be back from his shift soon, and Bud had probably woken up from his nap. He hoped Bud wouldn't say anything about what he'd walked in on. Even though he'd admitted to Bud that he was gay, he was sure Walter didn't know, and Lucky had no idea what to expect from him. The trailer was silent as he let himself back in. He was startled to see Bud sitting up in bed, watching TV. He seemed wide awake, his nap clearly having done him good. Lucky bit his lip and then sat on his bed, not knowing what to say.

"That was your fella?" Bud asked after a long moment of silence.

"Uh, yeah."

"Don't sweat it none, son," Bud said. "You two need some time alone, you just let me know."

Lucky couldn't believe his ears. He nodded silently. That seemed to be the end of the conversation, since Bud had turned his attention back to the baseball game on his TV. He had not expected their talk to go so well, and now he had a place he could come with Aaron if they wanted to be alone.

"Thanks," he said. He imagined coming back there as soon as he could swing it with Aaron, so they could pick up right where they'd left off.

"Where have you been?" Aaron asked as Lyn let herself into the kitchen. He had a pint of vanilla ice cream in his hand. Drowning his sorrows had seemed the best option available to him when he'd arrived at home. He'd been surprised that she was out; Lyn didn't usually go out without him. The fact that she'd gone without him made him feel even worse.

"The movies and then dinner with some friends," Lyn replied. "You just get home?"

Aaron shook his head and flipped absentmindedly through the apps on his phone. "Got home just in time for dinner with the parentals. All four of them." It had been sheer torture.

"Oh, no." Lyn put a comforting hand on his arm. "I'm sorry I wasn't here to be a buffer."

"It was fine, Lyn," Aaron muttered. "You can't be around twenty-four seven."

She still looked upset and guilty, so Aaron changed the subject. "What movie did you see?" He smiled as she took the bait and launched into a description of the movie she'd seen. "We stopped for burgers after." She paused. "Oh, and we ran into Lucky."

"You did?" Aaron panicked. *Had Lucky said anything? Did Lyn know now?*

"Yeah. He looked good. It's a shame you never hit that."

"Lyn!" His felt as if his face turned five different shades of red. Lyn just cackled. "I'm going to bed," Aaron said, getting up instead of replying. It would only encourage her, and there was a chance something he didn't want her to know might slip out.

"Don't do anything I wouldn't do," she teased. Aaron groaned and headed upstairs. He just wanted to go to bed and dream about Lucky.

Chapter Eleven

AARON BIT HIS LIP, PACING in the back of the church. He had no earthly clue how he'd ended up here. The face in the mirror stared back at him, mocking. It was the face of a stranger, of someone Aaron didn't know, and yet it was himself. Feeling he was choking, he straightened the bowtie around his neck. His future was approaching like an oncoming train, and he was tied to the tracks, unable to stop the train or escape. He'd tried, he really had, but it had been inevitable.

"You ready, son?" his father said. He was also dressed impeccably in a black tuxedo. "Wouldn't want to keep your bride waiting."

Aaron swallowed hard. This was actually happening, and there was nothing he could do to stop it. In just a few short minutes, he and Lyn would be married, and his life would be over. Marriage was supposed to be a new beginning for two people, but for Aaron, this wedding was a death sentence. His father put his hands on Aaron's shoulders, nearly pushing him out of the back room of the church and into the sanctuary. A crowd of hundreds seated in the pews had all eyes on him. Instrumental music played as Aaron walked to his proper place at the altar. His legs were shaking, and his heart was pounding. The idea that he could not do this reverberated through his very soul. He wanted nothing more than to run away, to hide from reality. This could not be his life.

One look from his mother, whose eyes watered as his best man—Richard Peterman, of course—led her down the aisle to her seat. Lyn's mother followed, escorted an usher who must have been a son of an important client or co-worker. The music changed as soon as she was seated. A flower girl came down the aisle, followed by three bridesmaids, all girls he and Lyn had gone to school with. He could hardly focus, instead spending the entire time trying not to hyperventilate. It was all Aaron could do to remain upright.

Then the *Wedding March* sounded through the speakers; the doors opened one last time to show Lyn in the doorway on her father's arm. She wore a gorgeous and insanely over-the-top white dress, presumably picked out by her mother. Her reassuring expression and delicate smile did nothing for his emotional state. She wasn't indifferent, but, like him, she was doing what was expected. It used to make him feel better about the whole thing–it had always been him and Lyn against the world.

Since meeting Lucky he couldn't even be around Lyn without feeling awful, and now they would be spending their lives together. Lyn and her father stopped in front of him. Her father lifted her veil and pressed a delicate kiss to her cheek before lowering it again. He took Lyn's hand from her father's, moving by rote. Everything had gone numb.

The pastor started speaking in a deep and booming voice. Aaron gripped Lyn's hand so tightly he had to be hurting her, but her expression never wavered. Her expression was serene, seemingly so sure. He bit his lip, wondering what was going through her mind. She was a good actress, but she'd never been this good before; he couldn't get a read on what she was thinking at all. Finally the pastor addressed the crowd, asking the question Aaron had been dreading.

"If any man has reason these two should not be wed today, let him speak now or forever hold his peace," the pastor said.

Aaron bit his tongue so hard he tasted blood. He wanted to speak up, to say that this was a farce, that he didn't love Lyn that way and he never would and then run for the hills. He didn't though; the disappointed faces of his parents and hers flashed before his eyes. The shocked gazes of the crowd watching them would be funny for about a moment, but his father's co-workers, employees and other important contacts were there. Speaking up was not an option.

"I have a reason!" a loud voice exclaimed from the back of the church. Aaron let out a gasp, seeing Lucky standing there at the end of the aisle, his curly hair bouncing. He wore jeans and a T-shirt, his beat up sneakers making scuffing noises on the carpet as he moved down the aisle. Aaron panted, his breath coming in sharp pains and he worked to get himself under control.

Lucky couldn't be here. Yet he was here and Aaron's heart was beating faster, hoping that Lucky had swooped in to take him away from all of this.

Aaron's father stood up. "Young man," he said, as if Lucky was a pebble in his shoe. "What is the meaning of this?"

Lucky's eyes never left Aaron's; he ignored Aaron's father as if he wasn't even there. Aaron had never seen someone ignore his father.

"Don't do this," Lucky said, clearly addressing Aaron. Gasps and whispers went through the crowd, and Aaron took in a sharp breath. "You don't love her. You love me."

"Lucky," Aaron managed to get out.

"Aaron?" Lyn asked. He met her wide-eyed gaze. She was clearly confused, and Aaron couldn't find the words to explain it to her.

"Aaron, please," Lucky interrupted. He held out a hand. "Come with me."

"Young man, this is preposterous!" Lyn's father had stood up now too, looking every bit as put out as his own father. Still, Lucky didn't acknowledge that anyone other than Aaron existed.

"Aaron, don't," Lyn said, but Aaron couldn't take his eyes off Lucky and his outstretched hand. Could he take it? Could he just go with Lucky and be free? Did he have the strength to walk away?

"I love you." Lucky spoke softly but clearly. "Aaron." He waved the fingers of the hand he held out, gesturing for Aaron to take it. Aaron moved toward Lucky, pulling his hands out of Lyn's grasp. She struggled to keep her grip, but Aaron's mind was made up. He couldn't marry her, not when Lucky stood there professing his love and asking Aaron not to go through with the wedding. Aaron's heart pounded as he moved, ignoring his father's booming voice as he shouted at them. Aaron didn't hear any of it, though. It was like listening to them under water. All that mattered was putting his hand in Lucky's and leaving with him.

"You can do it, Aaron," Lucky pleaded. "Walk away with me; you deserve to be happy."

"Aaron, don't," Lyn said, grabbing his arm. His eyes on Lucky, Aaron shrugged her off. He was so close, Lucky's hand was right there. He could almost reach it.

"Aaron," Lyn repeated his name. "Aaron, please."

Aaron reached out a hand for Lucky, willing his fingers to touch Lucky's. No matter how Aaron reached, their hands wouldn't connect.

"Lucky!" Aaron cried out. Why couldn't he reach Lucky?

"You can do it, Aaron." Lucky's voice echoed. "Break free."

"Aaron," Lyn shouted, shaking him. "Aaron, wake up!"

Aaron jerked upward, nearly bumping heads with Lyn. He was discombobulated, unsure of where he was or what was going on.

"Lyn?"

"Yes. Are you okay? You were shouting in your sleep. It sounded like you were being murdered or something."

"I–I'm fine," Aaron muttered. He wasn't fine, and she obviously didn't believe him, based on the expression on her face. "Nightmare." He tried to force himself to smile but he didn't quite succeed.

"I wish you'd just talk to me," she whispered. "We tell each other everything. We used to, anyway."

"I know." Aaron couldn't look at her; he clutched the bed sheets. The urge to be sick washed over him–the strain on their relationship was his fault. "I–I want to."

"Then just tell me," Lyn pleaded. "I'm your best friend."

"You are. I just… I need more time."

She sighed, getting up from where she was perched on the side of his bed. "Okay." Lyn paused in the doorway of his bedroom. "You know where I'll be."

* * *

Lucky was still surprised that Bud had reacted as he did. He was also mortified at being walked in on—he could barely speak to Bud without turning red in the face. He'd barely seen Aaron all week; Aaron had been just as embarrassed by the incident. Aaron had also been concerned that someone might find out—like his family—but Lucky had pointed out how unlikely that was, even if Bud mentioned it to someone. They'd still texted though, keeping up a steady stream of conversation about simple and mundane things and not about how they'd been discovered half-naked.

There was no talk of college or Aaron's family or the fact that summer was rapidly drawing to a close and they would both be leaving in just a few short weeks. There was no discussion of what would happen after they'd left this beach paradise and faced the real world. Lucky didn't know what he wanted, if he was honest. He'd fallen head over heels for Aaron, something he'd hoped for at the beginning of summer, but now he had a feeling it was all going to end in heartache. Aaron would be going off to Harvard, and he was going to Chicago, and there might as well be a million miles between them. He couldn't see that working out.

He hated it when his mother was right.

Bud entering the trailer disrupted his maudlin thoughts, and Lucky took in a deep breath.

"You okay, boy?" Bud asked, sitting on his bed.

"Fine." Lucky wondered if he could get up and leave without raising too much fuss.

"You look like someone killed your dog."

“I have a lot to deal with,” Lucky told him.

“This about that boy the other night?”

Lucky took a deep breath. “Sort of.” Bud gave him a look. Lucky sighed. “It’s complicated.”

“It always is. You kids these days got it so much better than when I was young, though.” Lucky looked at him in surprise. “You can be gay or whatever floats your boat and no one looks at you cross-eyed.”

“I wouldn’t go that far,” Lucky said.

“When I was your age being gay was a disease,” Bud told him. Lucky blinked. “The worst thing you could do was get caught with a guy. No telling what would happen if you were outed then. Many a friend of mine were injured by fists as much as words.”

Lucky couldn’t believe his ears. Could Bud be gay? Bud chuckled at his wide-eyed expression.

“But you’re married!” Lucky gestured at the wedding ring on Bud’s finger.

“Sure am,” Bud said, going quiet for a moment, as if he was collecting his thoughts. “Was different times back then. You got married. It was expected. We have two kids, older than you.”

“Aaron, my boyfriend, he’s still in the closet,” Lucky said. He hoped that Aaron wouldn’t be upset that Lucky was talking about him with Bud. “He says his parents wouldn’t understand.”

Bud nodded. “Some folks still don’t get it. They don’t want to.”

“But don’t you want to be yourself? Your *real* self?”

“That’s what you gotta realize, sonny,” Bud replied. “I am. I made decisions I could live with. That’s all any one can do.”

Lucky wasn’t sure what to think. He couldn’t imagine having to marry someone to keep up appearances, and he was so glad that the world wasn’t like that anymore. He could legally marry now and would never have to pretend to be someone he wasn’t.

“I am who I am,” Bud said. “I made those choices and I do love my wife, as much as I can.” He paused, then continued. “I don’t work this job cause the pay’s good.”

"*Oh*," Lucky exhaled. Of course. Bud traveled and that meant he was probably hardly ever home. Lucky wondered what his wife thought of that. "Does she know?" It was probably none of his business, but he had to ask.

"She's never said, directly, but I'm sure she's got an idea."

"Do you ever... with guys?" Lucky blurted out. This whole conversation had spun his head completely around. "Wow, I–" He silently cursed his inability to hold his tongue. "You don't have to answer that."

"I thought that's how it would be," Bud told him, almost as if he was admitting a deep, dark secret. "I figured, I could do that and who would it hurt?" He shook his head. "Turns out it would hurt me. Tried once or twice and couldn't do it. I made Agnes promises when I married her, and I keep my promises."

"Wow. That's awful."

"It's not that bad. You kids today, you got it so much better. Tell your fella that his family finding out ain't the end of the world. He's still got you."

Bud stood up, disappeared into the bathroom, and shut the door. Lucky stared after him, thinking. He couldn't imagine living a life like Bud's. It had to be such a lonely existence.

He sighed, his mind turning back to Aaron. He needed to see him.

Meet me at our spot?

Lucky waited for Aaron's return message. It didn't take long.

I'll be there as soon as I can.

Chapter Twelve

Aaron paced around the clearing, waiting for Lucky. They hadn't seen each other since his breakdown and the subsequent embarrassment. Aaron was just glad that Lucky's roommate had been cool about the whole thing—at least he assumed the man had been. Lucky hadn't said anything about it all week. They'd texted about mundane things instead, something Aaron had been glad of. He needed that break from the stress.

"Hey." Lucky's voice said behind him, and Aaron turned around.

"Hi."

Lucky crossed the clearing in three great strides, took Aaron into his arms, and kissed him soundly. Aaron gasped against Lucky's mouth and gripped Lucky's arms tightly. Lucky's arms were around his waist, holding Aaron snugly against him. Lucky's kiss was fierce and demanding; desire like Aaron had never known swept over him, and he stopped thinking. He gave himself over to Lucky's kisses, forgetting everything but the feel of Lucky's lips on his.

Lucky pulled back just long enough to pull his shirt over his head and throw it on the blanket they always used; Aaron had brought it and spread it out on the ground while he'd waited. Lucky pulled Aaron's shirt over his head, and Aaron barely had a second to process before

Lucky was on him again. Lucky tugged Aaron down onto the blanket. Aaron went willingly. Lucky covered his body with his own before Aaron could blink. He had no idea what had gotten into Lucky, but he didn't care.

He wasn't an idiot; he understood what desire was, and Aaron was definitely intimately acquainted with his right hand, so that was no mystery. Despite that, he had had no idea that he could feel like this with another person. He felt feverish and out of control, and it was absolutely perfect. He'd spent his whole life denying himself everything, and he wasn't going to deny himself this. The idea of life without Lucky swam into his thoughts, but Lucky's tongue exploring his chest drove it away. His need increased, something he hadn't imagined possible. All they had was here and now and he couldn't let this moment pass him by.

Lucky hadn't come to the clearing intending to get naked with Aaron, but that's exactly what happened. He was tempted to pinch himself, but he didn't want Aaron to see. They were quiet, wrapped up the blanket, and it was absolutely perfect. The smell of the salt in the air and the birds chirping in the trees added to the serenity of the moment. Aaron was tangled up in his arms and Lucky was intent on never letting him go. His hands couldn't stay still; they traveled over the skin of Aaron's back, traced the contours of his bicep, and then played with the wisps of Aaron's reddish brown locks.

"I never thought..." Aaron said softly.

"Never thought what?" Lucky asked. He tilted his head so he could see Aaron's face.

"That I would have… *this.* Any of this. *You.*"

"I hoped I would," Lucky told him. "I've wanted to feel this way about someone my whole life."

"Really?" Aaron scrunched up his nose, clearly trying to picture it.

"Yeah." Lucky let out a slightly embarrassed laugh. "Mama always told me I was ridiculous. She used to say that love like that didn't exist, that falling in love would just lead to a broken heart."

"Wow. Sounds like she had a bad break up."

"My dad left when I was little," Lucky said. "She didn't take it well."

"Oh," Aaron said. "My parents are still together. I think they love each other." Aaron sounded unsure, and Lucky's heart ached for him. He wasn't sure which was worse—his dad splitting or the idea of two parents in a loveless marriage.

"My mom was wrong, though," Lucky told Aaron.

"She was?"

"I met you, didn't I?" Lucky bit his lip, waiting for Aaron to say something. Aaron's eyes had gone wide. Lucky grinned. He very much liked it when he was able to shock Aaron.

"Same here," Aaron whispered, and Lucky swore his heart skipped a beat. Aaron loved him too. "Sometimes I think that I'll wake up one morning and all of this, *you*, it'll have been a really good dream."

Lucky couldn't resist. He pinched Aaron lightly on his back. Aaron startled. "Hey!" he exclaimed. Lucky laughed.

"Now you know it's not a dream."

"I guess I do," Aaron said, smiling.

"Your smile is beautiful," Lucky said, tracing a fingertip along Aaron's cheek. He could feel stubble and shivered at the sensation. Aaron blushed.

"I hate to say this," Aaron spoke up, "but I should go soon."

"Do you have to?"

"Probably. I'm sure everyone is wondering where I am." Aaron moved to sit up. "Though I'm not sure I can get dressed…" he trailed off and Lucky followed his gaze under the blanket. Evidence of their time together was clear on both of them and Lucky wasn't sure he wanted to put his clothes on over that either.

"I have an idea," he told Aaron.

They dressed only in their underwear, Aaron's face burned as they trekked through the woods with the blanket wrapped around their nearly naked forms. Lucky led them out of the tree line and onto the beach, getting as close to the water as he dared before losing the blanket and dropping his clothes on it. He wasted no time wading into the water and turned around to motion Aaron in after him. Aaron gave him a disbelieving look and then laughed and copied him.

Lucky pulled Aaron toward him as soon as he was close enough to reach. He wrapped his arms around Aaron's waist, enjoying the sun and the waves as they bobbed together in the water. The sun was setting, casting everything in a rosy glow.

"I couldn't have imagined a more perfect day than this," Aaron said in his ear. Lucky shivered.

"We'll just have to have another one tomorrow."

"I hope so."

They were quiet, exchanging chaste kisses, letting the water wash them clean as they stood among the waves.

THE SUN MOVED LOWER IN the sky, and Aaron shivered in Lucky's arms as a cool breeze swept over the water. With unspoken agreement they headed for the beach with their hands clasped tightly. They separated long enough to slip their clothes back on, drying off as much as they could. Aaron checked his shorts pocket for his phone.

Crap. He had ten missed texts from Lyn and another slew of missed calls.

He skipped the missed phone calls and went straight to the texts from Lyn.

Where are you? Dinner with the 'rents and Petermans.

Aaron, seriously, you're late

Are you really not coming?

Your dad is going to freak out

Text me so I know you're not dead in a ditch somewhere

Talked the 'rents into going without us

*Parentals not pleased—*you *owe me*

Tell me you're at least getting lucky.

Hah. Getting Lucky. Hahahahahaha.

Aaron nearly dropped his phone at the last one.

"Everything okay?" Lucky asked. Aaron could only nod, his face burning in mortification.

"Walk me home?" Aaron asked. The question slipped out before he could stop it, but he didn't want to take it back. His parents were out, and he wasn't ready to say good-bye to Lucky, wasn't ready to leave this absolutely amazing day for the real world. He wanted to live in the moment forever, relishing the feel of Lucky's hands on his skin and Lucky's lips on his.

"You sure?" Lucky asked, his voice low and breathy. This was a big deal, and Aaron loved that Lucky realized it. Lucky slipped his arm around Aaron's shoulders as they headed up the beach. Aaron clutched the blankets to his chest as they walked, snuggling into Lucky's side. No, this wasn't a public declaration, exactly, but it was close. It was time that Lyn knew.

The walk was short, and Aaron sighed when his house came into view.

"You sure you're okay?" Lucky asked, concern in his eyes.

"Yeah. I just don't want this to end." That was loaded statement—he didn't want this thing with Lucky to end, he didn't want the summer to end, he didn't want his real life to kill the joy and love he'd experienced today.

"I know the feeling," Lucky said as they headed up into the yard. Aaron put the blankets on the lounge chair on the porch and then turned to face Lucky.

"I'll call you before I go to bed," Lucky said.

Aaron nodded, suddenly unable to find words. How did he even begin to tell Lucky how much the entire day had meant to him? He stared into Lucky's eyes. The emotions in Lucky's gaze matched the ones spiraling inside him. Aaron took a half step, then leaned up just a hair and kissed Lucky softy but firmly. Lucky pulled him close. He kissed him harder before pulling back a little. Aaron was breathless.

"Good night," he whispered.

"Good night," Lucky whispered back. He untangled himself from Aaron, and picked up the blankets. Smiling so hard it hurt his face, Aaron watched him walk away. Lucky waved before he disappeared down the beach, and Aaron waved back.

He sank into the patio chair and let out a deep breath.

Holy crap.

"Aaron Ledbetter." Aaron's head snapped up at Lyn's voice. He met her disbelieving gaze, and his stomach dropped to his shoes, somersaulting the whole way.

"Lyn." He knew she'd be there, knew she'd see, but he was still nervous.

"You got some 'splainin' to do," Lyn said, crossing the porch to take the seat across from him. Her voice was full of emotion that Aaron couldn't read. He didn't know where to begin. She must have seen the conflict in his eyes, because her gaze softened. "You can start with telling me if that kiss was as toe-curling as it looked."

Aaron's cheeks burned red again, but relief shot through him. He bit his lip and slowly nodded his answer to her question. Lyn let out a loud, unladylike squeal, one that nearly ruptured an eardrum. He was sure her parents had no idea she could make a sound like that.

"I am such an idiot!" she exclaimed, slapping a hand on her forehead. "Of course you've got a boyfriend. Nothing else would have made you act the way you have been the last few weeks. I can't believe I didn't see it sooner! I must be slipping."

Aaron debated trying to get a word in edgewise, but figured that silence was probably his best option. He was just so, so immensely glad that she didn't seem to be hurt or angry about him not telling her sooner.

"I'm going to need details, my friend," Lyn told him, taking him by the arm and pulling him into the house. "Start at the beginning and don't you dare leave anything out."

Chapter Thirteen

Lucky was floating on cloud nine. While the way it happened was unexpected, he'd daydreamed about that moment more than he'd admit to anyone. He certainly hadn't expected to feel the way he was feeling now—so sure of his feelings, so sure of Aaron. Maybe it wasn't such a big deal that he and Aaron would be off to different colleges in a matter of weeks. They loved each other, they could try to make it work, couldn't they? Other people had long distance relationships. Hell, Bud was gay and still managed to make it work long distance with his wife.

Lucky let his feelings drown out his nagging doubt. He wanted to replay every moment. He wanted so much to draw what had occurred that his skin itched with the urge. The need to capture every moment was all-encompassing.

His phone buzzed with an incoming text as he let himself into the trailer. It was a text from Aaron.

I told Lyn about us.

Lucky smiled so wide he his face nearly cracked. He wasn't a secret anymore. Even more reason to think that they had the beginnings of something great and could make it work.

And?

He got out his pencils and paper while waiting for Aaron's reply, then sat cross-legged on his bed with his sketchpad in his lap and his phone next to him.

She's freaking out.

She keeps smacking me for not telling her sooner

I think she left a bruise

She says if you hurt me she's going to hunt you down

Lucky laughed and shook his head. Lyn was something else; he knew that despite the little time they'd spent together.

Duly noted.

I'll kiss any bruises better...

A moment passed without a reply from Aaron, and Lucky picked up his pencil, pressing the tip lightly onto the paper, beginning to sketch the way Aaron had looked last night, lying in his arms. He hoped he could do it justice. He needed desperately to get the pictures in his mind down before they faded, though he wasn't sure he'd forget the way Aaron had looked lost in ecstasy any time soon. Maybe he'd gone too far in his text to Aaron; it took him a little while to answer, but soon his phone indicated a new message.

When can I see you again?

Lucky gave a happy sigh at that text and typed a quick reply. He couldn't wait to see Aaron again.

Aaron had been silly not telling Lyn about Lucky sooner. Yeah, he had to put up with her giving him all kinds of crap and teasing him mercilessly, but he finally had someone to discuss things with, someone who could tell him if he was crazy for feeling what he was feeling and so soon, someone to tell him if he was deluding himself by staying in this relationship with Lucky. They'd already discussed more than Aaron had imagined telling her, but that's what he loved about Lyn, that he could tell her anything.

Going on and on about a boy to her, giggling like mad and smiling so much his face hurt—these were all things he'd dreamed about growing up.

There was also an angle he hadn't considered that made him feel like an idiot. With Lyn in the loop, he had someone who could help him sneak away to be with Lucky. There was only so much longer that he could continue to use his jogging excuse and expect his parents to keep believing him. With Lyn as a cover, he could pretend he was out with her and neither set of parents would have reason to suspect otherwise.

He loved that plan, and of course Lyn was game for it. It was as if distance between them of the last few weeks had never happened, with both of them planning excursions, dates, and cover stories so Aaron could see Lucky as much as Lucky's work schedule would allow. His and Lyn's relationship was back on track, and Aaron was glad; he'd missed her.

The only dim spot was the chewing out his father gave him when the parentals returned from dinner. More than just being late, Aaron had missed a social obligation. In the past, Aaron wouldn't have dreamed of it. He was supposed to feel guilty about it, supposed to grovel at his father's feet during the hour-long lecture about being a man of his word.

Instead, he was focused on Lucky and how he and Lyn could work it out so Aaron would see Lucky next time. He was sure his cursory apology to his father and his lack of an explanation of his whereabouts wasn't enough for his father, but Aaron didn't care.

He'd finally found something he wanted more than his father's love and approval.

If only Aaron had the nerve to tell him that.

Lucky was not expecting the text he got from Aaron.

Come hang on the beach with me and Lyn.

His eyes widened, and he bit his lip. This was a big deal—after all, Lyn was Aaron's best friend. On the other hand, he happened to have the trailer all to himself for the night, thanks to Bud and Walter having to work the late shift. The idea of having Aaron over took hold of him.

Sure… unless you want to come here??

Heart pounding with anticipation, he sent back his reply. He wanted to see Aaron again, to touch him and taste him. He was pretty sure that he would never get enough of it, but he definitely wanted to find out. He could only hope that Aaron felt the same way.

Alone?

Lucky smiled.

Until midnight.

Almost holding his breath, Lucky waited for Aaron to respond. He glanced around the room for a distraction and sighed. He could call his mother, but that was the last thing he wanted to be doing if Aaron was on his way. Also, he'd be tempted to tell her everything, and Lucky didn't want her raining on his parade. She'd been hurt, but that didn't make her an expert on all men. She didn't know Aaron, didn't know how much he and Aaron loved each other. They would find a way to make it work. Other people did; they could too.

On my way.

Lucky grinned when he got Aaron's final text. He darted around the room, straightening up as much as he could before turning down his narrow bed. That done, he sat on the edge of the bed, wondering how soon Aaron would be there and if it was possible he might explode from anticipation. He rubbed his hands together; his time would be much better spent putting pencil to paper. He grabbed his sketchpad and started drawing; the charcoal smudged his fingers as he moved it across the paper. He let himself simply draw, allowing his hand to make its own path across the paper, letting the dark lines flow gracefully. He drew diligently, losing himself and nearly forgetting that Aaron was on his way. In fact, Aaron's soft knock on the door of the trailer made him jump.

He stared at the sketchpad for a second and then shook his head. Even abstractly, he was still drawing Aaron. He flipped the pad closed and put down his charcoal, then wiped his hands on a rag as he went to answer the door.

Aaron's smiling face peered up at him, and Lucky couldn't help but grin in response. He stood back and let Aaron inside, nearly melting when he caught a whiff of Aaron's cologne. He had no idea what scent it might be, but it smelled delicious and was enough to make Lucky want to bury his head in Aaron's neck and just breathe him in. Lucky didn't though, figuring it bordered on creepy, and instead focused on Aaron who was now sitting on the edge of his bed. Aaron was alone with him in his room, *in his bed,* and they had hours before someone would be back.

It was absolutely perfect.

"What are you working on?" Aaron asked. He looked as nervous as Lucky himself. Just because they'd done certain things together before didn't mean they were going to be completely cavalier about everything. He went along with Aaron's questioning, thinking that it might help if they started talking and relaxed. Lucky sat next to Aaron on the bed; their thighs brushed as he shifted and he opened his sketchbook to show Aaron his work.

Aaron leaned over his shoulder to see, and Lucky could smell him again. Need thrummed under his skin and sung through his veins but he held back, wanting Aaron to be at ease. "It's mostly just sketches, pencil and charcoal."

Aaron took the pad and flipped through the pages; his eyes grew wide.

"They're all of me," Aaron said, sounding thunderstruck. Lucky smiled. "I can't seem to draw anything else these days. I draw what I love."

"Is that really how you see me?" he asked, running a finger lightly over one of the sketches.

"You don't?" Lucky said. Aaron shook his head slowly.

"You said you knew you were gay when you looked at piece of artwork online." Aaron changed the subject after a long moment. His eyes were full of emotions that Lucky couldn't name. Lucky nodded.

"Can I see it?" Lucky wasn't quite sure where this was going, but there was no reason not to show Aaron the piece.

"Sure," he agreed, pulling out his phone. He opened his Internet app and clicked on the link to the painting; he'd had it bookmarked for as long as he could remember. Lucky had spent a lot of time over the years staring at that painting. He turned his phone so Aaron could see it. Aaron's sharp intake of breath was loud in the otherwise silent room; his eyes were wide as he took in the painting.

"Oh, my," Aaron breathed out. "I get why seeing it made you realize you were gay."

He hadn't told that story to anyone but Aaron, and he still couldn't believe he'd done that. He was glad Aaron knew though, because Lucky loved the idea of sharing this painting with the world. It was gorgeous and more people needed to see it.

"What if..." Aaron trailed off, looking from the phone to Lucky and then back at the phone, his face bright red. Whatever he'd been about to say had clearly embarrassed him.

"What?" Lucky encouraged softly.

"Could you draw me?" Aaron whispered; he was so quiet. "Like that."

Lucky stared at Aaron. He wasn't sure he'd heard Aaron correctly.

"You want me to draw you like this?" He gestured to the artwork.

"Yeah," Aaron answered, his voice still soft. "Just like that."

Lucky swallowed hard, nearly choking. Aaron was asking to be drawn naked and in a pose that Lucky found extremely arousing. He nearly pinched himself, he was so sure he was dreaming; but Aaron was still sitting next to him. Aaron was still staring at him, wide-eyed and waiting for a reply.

"Draw me like one of your French girls," Aaron's voice was again quiet, but this time it had a teasing tone. Lucky chuckled at the *Titanic* reference and answered the only way he could. He said yes.

Aaron's hands shook as he undid the buttons at the collar of his polo shirt. He slipped the light blue material over his head slowly and tried not to freak out because Lucky was watching him undress. He chanced a glance at his boyfriend, and what he saw nearly took his breath away. Lucky was watching him with an intensity in his eyes that Aaron couldn't fathom. Tension filled the air as Lucky slipped off his sandals and then his belt. Lucky's hands suddenly tangled with his, and Aaron nearly swallowed his tongue. He locked gazes with Lucky, freezing under the power in his eyes. Lucky's hands continued working, unfastening Aaron's belt and then his shorts. The thin material of his khakis slid down his legs to the floor; the belt buckle clanked as it hit. Aaron barely heard it over the rapid pounding of his heart.

He couldn't believe he was doing this. He, Aaron Ledbetter, was about to pose nude for his artist boyfriend. Not even in Aaron's wildest fantasies had he ever imagined anything like this. He took a deep breath when Lucky's fingertips skimmed across his lower abdomen, resting lightly on the edge of his underwear. Lucky's fingers slipped under the elastic of the waistband, and Aaron didn't move as Lucky slipped off the garment. Aaron's underwear puddled on the floor on top of his shorts, and he carefully stepped forward over the pile of fabric. Lucky's hands trailed along his skin, sending shivers down his spine, until they found his hands. Lucky took both of Aaron's hand in his own and led him to the bed.

Aaron let Lucky settle him on the bed; Lucky moved Aaron around almost as if he was a doll. Aaron kept his arms and legs pliant as Lucky settled him into the correct pose. Aaron concentrated on his breathing and the feel of Lucky's hands on him, pushing away the fact that he was going to lie there, completely exposed, while Lucky drew him.

Lucky's hands trembled against Aaron's skin as he worked to pose Aaron as he wanted.

"Breathe, Lucky," Aaron said softly, glancing at Lucky to see his face. Lucky's eyes locked on his, and Aaron's lips curved into a slow smile. Lucky let out a chuckle and shook his head; his hair bounced lightly.

Finally, Lucky drew back and stared at him with what Aaron had come to call his "artist's face." Aaron probably should have felt exposed—after all, he was laid on the bed, arranged in a pose that Lucky found extremely erotic. And yet, a calm feeling flowed through him, taking away any anxiety. This was as much for him as it was for Lucky.

Aaron closed his eyes and let himself drift the moment Lucky put the tip of the pencil to the paper. The only sound in the room was the air conditioner, blowing loudly from its perch in the window. The white noise drowned everything else out. If Aaron wasn't so acutely aware of Lucky's presence, of Lucky's eyes on his body, Aaron might think was dreaming. After all, moments like this did not happen to him.

It seemed as if only minutes had passed when Lucky dropped the pencil. He wanted to open his eyes, wanted to ask Lucky if he was done, but Aaron didn't want to disturb the mood of the room if Lucky had more he wanted to do. His eyes shot open though, when Lucky's hand trailed up his bent thigh.

"You look..." Lucky trailed off. His brown eyes were wide and dark when Aaron stared into them. Lucky had never looked at him this intensely. His movements slow, Lucky knelt on the bed next to him. Desire rolled off him in waves, and Aaron wanted to grab him, pull Lucky down on top of him and kiss him senseless. He didn't though, but instead breathed deeply and let Lucky explore his body. Lucky's hands were slow and tentative as they passed over Aaron's skin. He paid special attention to Aaron's knees, the slope of his abdomen, the creases of his elbows, and the dip of his clavicle. Lucky's lips followed his hands, and Aaron let out a soft moan. His entire body hummed.

He needed Lucky and he needed him now or he was going to go insane.

He moved his arms then, wrapped them around Lucky's shoulders and pulled Lucky upward. Aaron pressed his lips to Lucky's.

"You're wearing too many clothes," Aaron said, grinning. He felt wicked and out of control and so unlike himself. He rolled them over precariously on the narrow bed, but he needed Lucky under him. Things turned frantic then, as both of them practically tore Lucky's clothes off.

"You have no idea," Lucky panted. "God, *Aaron*."

No one had ever spoken Aaron's name like that, not even Lucky, the last time he and Lucky were naked together.

Aaron liked it.

He wanted to hear it again.

"You, in *that* pose..." Lucky seemed unable to put together a complete sentence and Aaron loved it. He let his mouth trail up and down Lucky's body. His skin was salty under Aaron's tongue, and he couldn't get enough. Finally, Lucky's clothes were gone, and there was nothing between them.

"When are you leaving for school?"

It slipped out of Lucky's mouth before he could stop it; he probably shouldn't have brought it up just then. Not after how perfect the evening had been. Not after Aaron had fulfilled every fantasy he'd ever had about that sketch.

And yet, here they were now, with Lucky wishing he'd just kept his big mouth shut. He didn't want to talk about this even though, logically, they should. Talking about it made it real, and Lucky wasn't sure he was prepared to deal with reality. The entire summer had been like a dream, getting to do what he loved every day while spending all of his free time with Aaron. He never wanted that to end. As excited as he was about college, moving to Chicago, and learning more about art, none of it would mean anything if Aaron wasn't in his life.

Aaron went stiff at his words, almost as if he was closing himself off physically. "About three weeks," he said. "You?"

"Same," Lucky replied, his voice rough and low with emotion.

"Are we…" Aaron trailed off, as if struggling to find words.

"I want to," Lucky said, pressing soft kisses to Aaron's eyes, cheeks, and even the tip of his nose. He understood what Aaron was trying to say.

"Chicago and Cambridge are pretty far apart," Aaron voiced the same doubts Lucky had been struggling with. "How will we…?"

"We can find a way to make it work." Lucky was so sure. He couldn't lose Aaron. He'd finally found his muse and his true love and they were the same person. So few people were that, well, lucky.

"You think so?" Aaron propped his head up on his hand with his elbow resting on the bed as he looked at Lucky. There was doubt in Aaron's eyes, and Lucky wanted nothing more than to make it go away.

"Of course we can," Lucky insisted. "There's email and Skype and a million other ways to stay in contact."

Aaron bit his lip. "But what about… this?" he asked, his free hand trailing along Lucky's arm. Lucky shivered under his touch. Aaron had a point. Not being able to touch Aaron like his whenever he wanted would be difficult.

"I'm not going to lie, Aaron. It won't be easy. Not even remotely." He paused. "But it would be worth it to be with you, to know that eventually we can have this, if we just get through the rough parts."

"Wow. I… I never imagined I'd have this, you know." Lucky stayed silent, letting Aaron gather his thoughts. "This, being with you, is more than anything I could have ever imagined."

Aaron went quiet, and Lucky enjoyed simply staring at him.

"You can keep telling me how awesome I am," Lucky teased. Aaron cracked a smile and Lucky let out a chuckle to ease the tension. "We'll work it out, Aaron, I promise."

It wasn't until Aaron had left to go back to his house that it occurred to Lucky: Aaron had never agreed with him.

When Aaron got back to the beach house, he found Lynn sitting on the porch, sipping hot chocolate. She had a blanket on her lap, and her phone was on the table. Her eyes were downcast and she quickly swiped at her cheek. He was immediately worried; he couldn't remember the last time he'd seen Lyn cry.

"You okay?" Aaron asked, walking up the steps.

"What?" Lynn glanced up at him, clearly startled. "I'm fine."

"You don't look fine. I know I've been preoccupied this summer, but you can talk to me too, you know."

She smiled, but it was forced. He was immediately unsettled. Lyn had never faked a smile with him. "It's nothing, Aaron, I promise."

He didn't believed her, but he couldn't force her to tell him what was wrong. He had no clue; maybe she was like him, dreading the end of summer and the end of their freedom. It was rapidly approaching, and no matter what Lucky said, they were probably kidding themselves about making their relationship last beyond the end of August. He sat in the chair across from her and let the sound of the ocean soothe him.

"How was your date?" Lynn gave him a teasing smile. Aaron couldn't help but smile back as he launched into the story. He left out some of the more intense moments, but Lynn still gasped when he talked about Lucky drawing him.

"He wants to make this work," Aaron told her. "He wants us to be together after we go off to school."

Lyn put her hand over her mouth and looked at him with an emotion in her eyes that Aaron couldn't name. "That's great. I'm so happy for you."

"I nearly passed out when he told me."

"He loves you," Lyn said with certainty. "Of course he would want to be together."

"It's long distance, Lyn. And with everything else…" he trailed off, gesturing between them. "You know it can't work."

"You won't know unless you try. It's not like I'm going to be a jealous wife, Aaron."

"I know that, but…"

"Oh my God," Lyn said a second later, staring at him with wide eyes.

"What?"

"He doesn't know, does he?" Lyn asked. "About us."

"There is no 'us,' Lyn."

"He doesn't know we're going to get married one day," Lyn said. "You haven't told him."

"No. He doesn't know."

"Aaron!" she exclaimed, hitting him hard on the arm. "How could you not tell him?"

"What was I supposed to say, Lyn? 'I really like you, Lucky, and I'd like a future together, but I've gotta marry my best friend to please my parents and hers, but really, it's nothing. You don't mind, right?'" He shook his head. "Lucky would do what any sane person would do and hightail it out of this relationship faster than I could blink."

"So lying to him makes it better?"

Aaron sighed. "Look, I've thought a lot about this. We're not getting married for a while. I'll tell Lucky when that gets… closer to being reality. We're probably not going to stay together after this summer anyway."

Aaron's heart hurt just thinking those words, and it was a struggle saying them out loud. Lucky's words, his promises to Aaron that they would work it out, were so tempting. He wanted to believe them, wanted nothing more than to be with Lucky. Aaron was beginning to find it impossible to imagine a future without Lucky in it, but he had to. One of them had to be realistic.

Lyn put a hand on his arm, and Aaron smiled sadly. "At least I know what love is now, right?"

"Oh, Aaron."

The sound of waves filled the silence between them, and Aaron wished that he could just slip into the ocean and let it carry him away.

Chapter Fourteen

LUCKY HUMMED HAPPILY UNDER HIS breath as he got ready for work the next day. Bud gave him a cursory glance or two, probably wondering what he was so happy about, but Lucky didn't care. He and Aaron were going to stay together; they were going to make this work. He was even more excited now, ready for his life to begin.

Lucky sighed when his mother's ringtone filled the air. He almost let it go to voicemail, but he was better off answering it. He loved his mother, but it was hard to put up with her negativity when he was so happy. On the other hand, purposefully ignoring her call would make him feel guilty.

"Mama, hi."

"Hello, Jonas," she replied. "You haven't called in a few days."

"I know." He'd been so wrapped up in work and Aaron that calling her hadn't been on his list of priorities. "I'm sorry. It's been so busy here—"

"You mean you've been spending all your time with that boy," Dinah said.

Lucky sighed.

"Mom, he's not just some guy." No guy would ever be good enough; no guy would ever be different from his father. "And I've been working; the carnival has been packed with people all summer."

"You listen here, Jonas," his mother interrupted. "I know you think that he's the best ever and he's gonna love you until the day you die."

Lucky bit his lip. Yeah, he was pretty much hoping that was the case, but he'd never tell her that.

"You're only eighteen and you have a lot of life left to live before you settle down," Dinah continued. "I'm not telling you this to hurt you, but you need to be realistic."

"Enough, Mama!" Lucky snapped. "How about having a little faith in me, for once?" His mother fell silent, clearly startled by his tone and his words. "I mean, damn it, Mama, I'm not stupid. I know what Dad did to you was shitty and I know you don't want me to end up hurt, but I can't not feel things the way you do!"

There was silence on the other end of the phone, and Lucky had a very good inkling that he'd gone too far.

"Mama, I'm sorry, I just…" he stumbled over his words. "Say something, please?"

"I think you've made it very clear that you don't want to hear anything I have to say."

Lucky's heart sank. He hadn't wanted to hurt her, just make her stop.

"When he breaks your heart, I won't say 'I told you so,'" she added.

Lucky rolled his eyes. "Goodbye, Mama." He hung up without waiting for her reply and then tossed his phone onto the bed. He was not in the mood to go into work now, to deal with all the screaming kids and annoyed parents. He wanted to climb into bed next to Aaron, pull the covers over their heads, and shut out the world, but he couldn't.

With another sigh, he picked up his phone, shoved it in his pocket, and headed out the door for the carnival.

"If you'll excuse me, I think I'll take a walk on the pier."

Aaron stood up from his seat. He'd had enough of his parents for the night. Since they'd sat down to dinner, it had been one veiled comment about him and Lyn and their upcoming futures, from school to the wedding and everything in between, after another. He'd had about enough when they started talking about honeymoon destinations. When they segued into baby names, Aaron couldn't keep calm any longer. He had to get out of there. If he stayed, he wasn't sure what he'd say or do, and he'd spent all summer trying to keep his parents from finding out about Lucky. Getting into a screaming match about him with his parents over dinner was probably not the way to go about bringing Lucky up for the first time.

"Don't stay out too late," his mother said. He nodded in agreement, avoiding Lyn's sympathetic gaze. Aaron just wanted to get of there, to see Lucky and forget for a while.

"Lyn, dear, why don't you join him?"

Aaron froze, steps from *escape* when Lyn's mother spoke. He groaned internally; he'd been so close. If Lyn came along, he would not be showing up at Lucky's trailer.

"Sure," Lyn replied after a second. She knew he didn't want her along, but he recognized that she didn't know how to get out of it. Lyn glanced at him, a neutral expression on her face as she took his arm, letting him drape her light sweater around her shoulders.

Aaron couldn't bring himself to say anything as they headed down the beach toward the pier. The lights from the carnival shone brightly in the dark. The pier itself didn't look terribly crowded—most people seemed to be at the carnival. The walk was quiet. Neither of them seemed to know what to say. The future that they had talked about for so long had always seemed like a far off thing, almost as if it would never come. Now it was upon them, and Aaron was freaking out.

The last thing he expected was to see Lucky sitting at the end of the pier, under the shelter house, staring off into the darkness over the ocean. Lyn nudged him, and Aaron glanced at her. She jerked her head in Lucky's direction, and Aaron bit his lip. Lyn made her way to a nearby bench and took out her phone. She'd been melancholy all day; the two of them were slightly less lively than a pair of goldfish.

"Hey," Aaron said, feeling awkward as he approached Lucky.

"Hey," Lucky replied. "I wasn't expecting to run into you."

"Lyn and I went for a walk," Aaron said, motioning to Lyn before sitting next to Lucky. He wanted to snuggle up into Lucky's side and wrap his arms around Lucky's neck, but he didn't. Aaron couldn't do that, not here, not where someone might see.

"I love the ocean," Aaron said, because he couldn't think of anything else to say. "Especially at night."

"You can't even see it," Lucky said.

"But you can hear it, and you can feel it and you can smell it."

"Hmmm." Lucky gave him a look. Lucky's artistic sensibilities probably wouldn't grasp the beauty of something that couldn't be seen with the naked eye. Lucky stood up and held his hand out for Aaron. Aaron debated, glancing around to see if there was anyone he might know.

"I won't bite, you know," Lucky murmured. "Unless asked." He leered a little and Aaron shook his head at Lucky's teasing, then took Lucky's hand before he could talk himself out of it. He let Lucky lead him to the edge of the pier. They leaned on the railing, standing as close to each other as they could, staring out at the water.

Aaron grinned so hard his face hurt. He'd dreamed about many a night like this, standing out on this very pier with a guy he loved, enjoying the night air and the sound of the ocean waves crashing into the surf.

"What?" Lucky asked quietly.

"I've just… always wanted to do this," Aaron said. "Come out here and walk with a guy and just…"

"So we're fulfilling a fantasy here, then?"

"I guess so." Aaron smiled.

"Well, that makes us even." There was an edge to Lucky's words; he was obviously thinking of the night before, when Aaron had been posed just so and Lucky had drawn his body, first with his pencil and then with his fingers. Aaron nearly moaned out loud thinking about it, and judging by the sound of Lucky's breathing, Lucky was having trouble controlling his thoughts as well.

A text tone rang out, and Aaron sighed. It was Lyn reminding him they had to get back soon.

"I have to go," Aaron said, pulling his hand way from Lucky's. "Lyn and I have to get back." He took a deep breath and a huge risk and kissed Lucky's cheek. Aaron turned to walk away, but Lucky grabbed him by the arm. Startled, Aaron started to speak, but Lucky's lips on his stopped anything he was going to say right in its tracks. Lucky's lips caressed his gently but firmly, taking and giving, until finally Lucky pulled away. They were both breathing heavily.

"Figured that was part of your fantasy," Lucky said.

Aaron let out a shaky laugh. "It was," he admitted. "I'll text you later."

"I'm counting on it."

Aaron was glad for the walk back, since it gave him time to calm down before seeing their parents again. Lyn kept silent, staring at her phone repeatedly and frowning. He wanted to ask her about it, but she probably wouldn't tell him even if he did. Aaron planned to put everything out of his mind for at least one more night. He couldn't wait to get into bed and fall asleep—all of his dreams would be about that wonderful, spine-tingling, amazing kiss.

Chapter Fifteen

THE NEXT MORNING FOUND LUCKY perched at his booth, watching as the carnival goers passed him by. His booth was always slow in the mornings. Wanting to use their money on other things first, most people waited until late afternoon get pictures.. It gave him time to do his own work between customers and to think about Aaron in his free time. He was startled when Lyn plopped herself into the chair at his booth.

"I don't get men," she said, looking at her nails, apparently checking out her manicure.

"I'm not sure there's a good way for me to reply to that," Lucky said.

Lyn chuckled. "Probably not."

"Boy trouble?" he asked. Was she on the outs with the tall, dark, and handsome he'd seen her with a few weeks ago? He considered asking her, but decided it was none of his business.

"You could say that," Lyn muttered. She shook her head as if to clear her mind. "How are things with you and Aaron?"

"Fantastic, wonderful, great." Lucky couldn't help but gush. "I never thought I'd find someone like him, you know?"

"He's definitely one-of a kind," Lyn said. "He really loves you, you know."

"I know," Lucky said softly. No matter what else may be up in the air between him and Aaron, he knew that much.

"You know, our parents are throwing a Labor Day party at the end of the week, kind of a wrap-up to the summer. I'm sure Aaron would love it if you would come."

"You think? But he's not… out, to his parents. I wouldn't want to complicate things for him."

Lyn sighed. "I know, but I really do think he'd love it if you were there."

"Yeah?" Lucky wasn't sure. He didn't want to make Aaron uncomfortable, and they had never discussed Lucky meeting his parents.

"I'm sure having you there would make it a lot better for him," Lyn said. "Most of the guests will be old fuddie duddies our parents work with. It'd be nice to have a *friend* of ours there to hang out with."

"Well…" he trailed off, not missing her use of the word friend. He knew what that meant; he and Aaron would not be together as boyfriends at the party.

"Look, just think about it," Lyn said, getting up. "I have to go see a man about a dog or something."

Lucky laughed and waved at her as she walked off. Maybe he would go to the party. Maybe it was time he met Aaron's family—after all, if they were going to do this, going to take their relationship the distance, then they would need all the support they could get. They wouldn't be getting any from his mother, but that was another issue he didn't want to think about now. He pictured the look on Aaron's face, how happy he would be when Lucky walked in and surprised him.

Maybe he would go.

* * *

Aaron woke up late that morning and rolled out of bed while wiping the sleep from his eyes. He rushed through a shower and dressed, then headed downstairs for a late breakfast.

He was startled to find his father in the kitchen.

Charles Ledbetter was an intimidating man. Aaron loved him despite that. He tried to tell himself that the only reason his father put so much pressure on him was because his father loved him and wanted him to succeed. That explanation had worked for him in the past; Aaron had always believed that if he worked harder, proved himself over and over, then his father might show Aaron that he was worthwhile in his father's eyes.

Meeting Lucky had thrown a wrench into everything he'd ever known; he couldn't imagine having a relationship with Lucky and keeping it quiet while he played happy family with Lyn. He just couldn't. He'd learned that much, this summer. There would be no way to do that for the rest of his life. Aaron just wasn't sure he was brave enough to tell his parents the truth.

Not yet, anyway.

Heart pounding as he approached the table, Aaron steeled himself for a talk with his father. That had to be the only reason his father was here instead of off with Lyn's father.

"Good morning," Aaron greeted cautiously, grabbing a banana from the fruit basket on the counter and a blueberry muffin from the plastic container next to the stove.

"Have a seat, son," Charles said, taking a sip of coffee from his cup. Aaron swallowed, his stomach rolling.

If his father had somehow found out about him and Lucky… He dismissed that idea immediately, though; his father hadn't even been to the carnival.

"We are going to host a Labor Day party this Friday night," Charles began. "A way to wind up the summer and entertain our friends and clients. A proper send off for you before college."

Aaron paused mid-bite, staring at his father in surprise. He quickly chewed and swallowed. "That seems kind of last minute," Aaron pointed out. His parents normally planned things like this far in advance, just as the Fourth of July party had been, and it was really unlike them to do anything on a whim. He hesitated to ask what was really going on. He wasn't sure he'd like the answer.

"It is, but we're sure we'll have an excellent turn out."

"Oh?" Aaron probed a little bit, trying to figure out exactly what the hell was going on. "Why is that?"

He took another bite from his muffin and nearly choked on it when his father put a small velvet jewelry box on the table between them.

Aaron forced himself to swallow and gasped in air. There could be only one thing in that box; his parents could only mean one thing by throwing an impromptu party.

He would be proposing to Lyn on Friday night.

Aaron couldn't move, could hardly breathe. His mind churned the same sentence over and over.

Not yet. I'm not ready yet. I need more time.

"Well, then," his father's voice penetrated his fog; Aaron must have spoken out loud. "Maybe you shouldn't have been kissing *that boy* where *anyone* could see you."

Aaron stared at his father, unable to formulate words. His worst fear since he was twelve and it was happening. *He knows, he knows, he knows...*

"John Peterman and his wife took a walk last night, too," Charles said. "And I must say, I was quite taken aback when he phoned me this morning to let me know what my son has been up to." Charles cleared his throat. "After I assured him that he was mistaken about what he witnessed, I invited him to the celebration of your engagement."

"Father, I—"

"I suggest you let me finish, son," Charles interrupted calmly. Too calmly. "Friday night, you will propose to Lyn. A wonderful surprise engagement. We'll celebrate the end of summer in style." His father rose, leaving the box on the table. "Whatever it is you think you're doing with that boy, Aaron, it ends now." Moments later, the front door opened and shut, and then Aaron was alone.

Somehow Aaron forced himself to pick up the ring box and stagger upstairs to his room. He shut and locked the door and sank onto his bed. He opened the box and stared at the ring. It was clearly expensive—only the best for Charles Ledbetter's son. He tried to picture the actual proposal and he was sick to his stomach. He couldn't do this to Lyn, to Lucky; he couldn't propose.

Couldn't *marry* her.

Then he imagined his parents faces if he refused. He lay back onto the bed and tried not to think.

Aaron stayed there the rest of the day. He declined both lunch and dinner, unable to handle the idea of food. He ignored Lucky's questioning texts when he failed to show up at the carnival as planned. He stared at the wall and wished he had another life where just being himself was good enough.

* * *

Lucky wasn't sure, but he had a feeling that Aaron was avoiding him. It was possible that Aaron was as busy as he said he was; Lucky just didn't think that was true. He wasn't sure if he should be upset because Aaron was lying to him, or just try to figure out exactly why Aaron was treating him as if he had the plague. They texted as they normally would, but when it came to seeing Aaron in person, it was as if Lucky had typhoid.

Playing it by ear seemed to be best. Whatever Aaron was dealing with would come out eventually—they were sure to talk again before they parted ways for school, unless this was Aaron's way of pulling away from him, of breaking up with him without having to face him. Lucky didn't want to think that, it was hard enough to think of being with Aaron long distance; he wasn't sure he could handle breaking up.

He debated talking to Aaron about it, but figured texting wasn't the best option for this serious discussion.

It was a very frustrating week and finally, Lucky was left with hoping they could sneak away on Friday to talk, really talk, about everything. They needed to decide how things were going to be.

He sighed as another customer approached his booth and talked to him about a drawing. As Lucky put pencil to paper, he silently urged Friday to hurry up.

Chapter Sixteen

Aaron stayed in his room all of Friday. His mother had insisted, once Aaron had complained of feeling sick to his stomach. That wasn't a lie either; every time he pictured the ring box in his bedside table drawer, he nearly threw up. His mother had sent him to bed to rest as a precaution; after all, it was going to be a "special night." This was completely okay with him; he wasn't sure he could handle his family or even Lyn without losing it completely. It was better that he stayed out of the way as he tried to figure out how he was going to make it through the night without causing a scandal.

He had no idea what their parents had told Lyn about the party. He was pretty sure she had no idea he was going to propose, and that made him feel even worse. She would be forced to say yes. He couldn't bring himself to face her, to warn her. It would make it all too real.

His phone buzzed. It was a text from Lucky, checking to see how he was doing. Aaron had texted him that he was under the weather, one of many excuses he'd used over the past week to keep from seeing Lucky. It wasn't that Aaron didn't want to see him. He wanted to see Lucky more than anything, wanted to be with Lucky more than anything. He just couldn't look Lucky in the eye and pretend everything was okay and then turn around and propose to Lyn.

Instead Aaron spent the day tossing and turning with a million thoughts jumbling in his brain. Half the time was spent planning his proposal speech for the party that night; he spent the other half imagining what it would be like to run off with Lucky and be happy for the rest of his life.

He didn't know what to do. No matter what he did, he would be disappointing someone he loved and hurting them.

Aaron had never felt so selfish.

He slipped on his white tuxedo with shaking hands. His parents had insisted on formal attire, of course. He sighed, staring into the mirror as he styled his hair. He took in his dead eyes and his expressionless face.

He was seconds away from punching the mirror when his father cleared his throat behind him.

"You ready, son?" Charles asked.

Aaron swallowed hard and nodded; Charles draped an arm around his shoulder. Aaron let his father lead him out of the bathroom and down to join their guests.

He finally understood that old saying: This was definitely the first day of the rest of his life.

It just wasn't the life he wanted.

It took Lucky one glance into the main room of Aaron's family's beach house to know he didn't fit in. He'd never been in a house that nice. Sure, he'd seen it from the outside, but lots of places on the beach were large. This one was large and opulent. Lucky was pretty sure the art hanging on the walls was worth more than his college education was going to cost. Wearing black dress pants and a white button-down shirt, he was out of place amongst partygoers in their tuxedos and evening gowns.

His lack of funds was no secret to Aaron though, so Lucky did his best to shrug off the uncomfortable feeling he had in the pit of his stomach. He focused on trying to find Lyn or Aaron. There were tons of people in the large space; their voices mixed with the warbling of a string quartet that was set up in the corner. Lucky spotted Aaron then, coming downstairs with a man who had to be his father. The resemblance between the two was uncanny. Aaron was practically edible in his white tux; Lucky had to swallow to keep his mouth from watering. That would not a good first impression make, especially since Aaron had said his relationship with his parents was complicated. Lucky hesitated near the wall, not sure if he should approach Aaron or wait for Aaron to find him. Surprising Aaron was the idea, but he didn't want to get Aaron in trouble with his parents either.

He stayed where he was, waiting to make his move when it wouldn't be so noticeable. He figured he could take a minute to meet the parents, and then he and Aaron could slip away to their spot. As good as Aaron looked in his tux, Lucky wanted nothing more than to get him out of it.

"Hey, you made it!"

Lucky turned to see Lyn, who was speaking up so he could hear her. He was startled but managed to keep his reaction in check. She was wearing a very daring white dress, one that crisscrossed over her breasts, revealing her toned and tanned stomach. The dress tied behind her neck; the bowstrings dangled down her back. There, on her shoulder, he saw what looked like a new tattoo. The edges of it were still raw and red.

"Yeah," Lucky replied. "Thought I'd surprise him."

"He'll be happy to see you," Lyn said. "He's been under the weather the last few days."

"So he said." Lucky eyed Aaron critically. He didn't look sick. A little down, maybe, but that was probably because he was talking to his father and nodding at every other word that came out of Mr. Ledbetter's mouth. Lucky supposed Aaron was a little paler than usual, despite his gorgeously tanned skin.

"He puts too much on himself," Lyn said, frowning.

"He does. He told me about Harvard, how he doesn't want to go."

Lyn just sighed and shook her head. "Don't say that too loudly around here. It's akin to sacrilege. Lightening might strike you or something."

“I won’t,” he promised, moving his finger over his heart in the shape of an X. Lyn grinned, took him by the arm, and headed for the kitchen where there were drinks.

“Take a drink,” she said, and handed him a bottle of sparkling water. “Head outside, I’ll send Aaron out as soon as I can.”

“Okay.” Lucky took the drink and sat in one of the deck chairs. The wind blew off the ocean, putting a chill in the air. Lucky didn’t mind the temperature, though it only reinforced that, after Monday, he and Aaron would have to go their separate ways for a while. He was glad Lyn was willing to help them get some time alone together. He took a sip of his water and leaned back in the chair, enjoying the music drifting outside from the party and the smell of the saltwater in the air. As soon as Lyn stole Aaron away, it would be perfect.

Aaron was relieved when Lyn pulled him away from his father to make the round of the room, until he took in what she was wearing. “Lyn, what the hell?” he whispered hotly.

“Are you trying to tell me I look bad?” she asked.

“You know you don’t,” he shot back. He gasped, reaching out to touch her left shoulder. “Lyn.” He traced the letters of the tattoo. “I know why the caged bird sings,” he read.

“It’s kind of our motto, right?”

“Your parents…” He couldn’t think. This was too much.

“I don’t care.” Lyn snapped. “I’m not a child anymore.”

Aaron glanced away, unable to think of anything to say to that. He locked eyes with his father and shivered. He read the look of warning on his father’s face, loud and clear. Aaron would be proposing tonight or there would be hell to pay.

He forced himself to make small talk with the guests as he and Lyn made their way through the crowd. The murmur of voices around them definitely increased as they took in Lyn, her dress, and her obvious tattoo. Oh, this would not end well. He could see concern on Lyn’s face out of the corner of his eye, so he did his best to make sure they were never alone. Finally she ushered him toward the patio door and outside. The railing was lined in twinkling lights, a beautiful sight, but he couldn't appreciate it; the next time he walked out onto the patio, he'd be an engaged man, just not to the person he wanted.

Lyn stared at him and then opened her mouth to speak, only to be interrupted by a familiar voice.

"Hey, y'all," Lucky's voice reached his ears, and Aaron closed his eyes. It was both music to his ears and the most horrible noise ever.

This isn't happening. Maybe if Aaron kept repeating that over and over in his head, it would be true. It would make it so that Lucky wasn't really standing there in front of him, not tonight. Not when he had to…

"What—" Aaron managed to get out. He shot a panicked look to Lyn, unable to say anything else.

"I invited him," Lyn said with a smile. Clearly, she'd thought she was doing him a favor. The color drained from Aaron's face, and he turned to see Lucky grinning at him, dressed in a white button-down and black slacks. It might not have been the latest fashion but he looked gorgeous, and Aaron bit his lip before he could groan out loud. "I know you guys only have limited time left to see each other." She kissed him on the cheek and disappeared inside the open patio doors.

"Hi," Lucky said softly.

Aaron couldn't help but smile back, even though he felt as though he might vomit.

"Hi." Aaron had no idea what else to say. He couldn't believe Lyn had done this. She'd dragged him into her rebellion, and he would have to deal with the fallout.

"So this is how you deal with being sick," Lucky observed with a drawl, keeping his voice low. It sent shivers down Aaron's spine, and he longed to feel Lucky's lips against his again. He couldn't though—not here, not now.

Not ever again.

"Not exactly. My parents..." Aaron trailed off, feeling guilty yet again. He was so damn tired of feeling awful all the time, but he couldn't seem to change it either. Aaron had no idea where to even begin.

The hardest thing about this whole mess was not only losing Lucky from his life, but accepting that he was never going to have the relationship he wanted, ever. He would marry Lyn and be faithful to her, because sneaking around and hiding wasn't something he could do any longer.

Aaron had never actually hated his parents before, but he did at that moment. It wasn't a feeling he liked. He'd wanted so much to make them proud of him, to do the things they asked because they were his parents and they wanted what was best for him. The realization that, if they really wanted what was best for him, they wouldn't make him do this hit him hard. He wanted to tear down the beach in a dead run, dragging Lucky with him, and never look back.

His father chose that moment to step out onto the patio.

Aaron nearly choked on his tongue. His eyes went wide, and Lucky gave him a questioning look.

"Dad." He somehow found the air to force the word out.

"Aaron, it's time," Charles said. "The last of our guests have arrived."

Aaron couldn't breathe.

"Mr. Ledbetter," Lucky said, holding out a hand for introduction. "I just wanted to introduce myself, I'm..."

"I know who you are," Charles said. His tone was cool but not confrontational. Lucky dropped his hand.

"Lyn invited him," Aaron found himself blurting out. Charles shot him a look that said he thought otherwise. "But he was just leaving."

"Nonsense," Charles replied, a hard edge to his voice belying his words. "Any friend of Lyn's is more than welcome."

Lucky's questioning gaze landed on Aaron, and Aaron sent him a pleading glance. Lucky needed to go before this got any worse; before Aaron had to get down on one knee and propose in front of the whole crowd.

"Thank you, sir," Lucky said with a smile.

"Things are just about to get exciting," Charles continued, looking at Aaron again. "Why don't you boys come in and see."

Aaron wanted to lash out, to shout his protest, to cause a scene, anything to delay the inevitable. His body no longer seemed to be under his control, and he found himself unable to do anything. How he managed to follow them inside, Aaron didn't know. His entire body had gone numb.

"Attention, everyone!" Aaron's father's voice rang out. Aaron's right hand went to the ring box nestled in his pocket. He was out of time, Lucky was *there*, and he hadn't explained *anything*.

"You should go," he hissed at Lucky under his breath. He didn't care what his father said. Lucky shouldn't have to see this. "*Please*."

"Why?" Lucky asked, though, judging by his expression, he thought he knew. He thought Aaron was panicking about his sexuality being discovered. If only he knew the truth…

"Lucky, please," he pleaded while his father continued to talk, going on about freedom and capitalism and who knew what else.

"Aaron, come up here, son!" Charles called. Aaron's eyes flew open wide and his mouth went dry. This was it. *Oh God.*

Somehow his legs moved and he turned away from Lucky, heading toward his father in the center of the room, even as he mumbled, "I'm sorry," in Lucky's direction. It would be an empty sentiment, yet he couldn't help but say it. The crowd parted for him, and he could only hope that Lucky had listened and left. He couldn't worry about that any longer though; it was out of his hands and it always had been.

He just hadn't realized that until now.

Aaron forced a smile as he turned to face the crowd. He noted that all the guests were friends and clients of his parents. This was it. There was no turning back.

"Thank you all for joining us," Aaron finally found his voice. "It means so much that you could be here to witness what will undoubtedly be the happiest night of my life." The words nearly stuck in his throat, and Lyn was giving him a panicked look; she'd just figured out what was going on. There were tears in the corners of her eyes, and her mouth was pinched at the corners. She was staring out into the crowd of partygoers as if one of them might save her from this fate. He led her to the center of the room. Aaron sank to one knee, barely avoiding collapsing to the floor in a heap. There would be time to fall apart later, when everyone was gone. He pulled the ring box out of his pocket. His heart was pounding his ears and his stomach was turning somersaults, but he had to keep going. "Evelyn Rossman, would you do me the honor of being my wife?"

"Oh, Aaron." Lyn breathed out. She looked pale and shaken, as if she'd rather do anything else than marry him. "This is so unexpected." His gaze met hers, and she could see the emotions in his eyes. He wasn't sure what he saw in hers, but she stood there so long, he wondered if she'd give him an answer.

"No."

The word was spoken quietly, but in the silence of the room, she might as well have shouted it.

Aaron blinked at her, wondering if he'd hallucinated.

"I'm sorry, Aaron, but no."

Aaron's mouth fell open. He had no idea what to do, or what to say. In all his thoughts of the future, he never once thought that Lyn would refuse to marry *him*. He stood on shaky legs. The crowd was chattering at fever pitch, the fact that Evelyn Rossman had just turned down Aaron Ledbetter's marriage proposal was too shocking to discuss quietly.

She pressed a chaste kiss to his cheek and then slipped through the crowd before any of the parentals could move. Aaron could barely register what had happened and stared blankly into the crowd around him.

"Go after her!" Aaron's father snapped, shoving Aaron roughly in Lyn's direction. He heard his father begin some sort of spin for the guests, as Aaron pushed blindly through the people around him. All he knew was that Lyn had just turned everything on its ear and that it wasn't her that he needed to find. It was Lucky. He had to explain everything to Lucky; he had to make him understand.

He had to make Lucky forgive him.

LUCKY DIDN'T KNOW WHAT TO do with himself. The scene from the party played over and over in his mind, like an evil torture. He couldn't quiet his thoughts. If Aaron had actually proposed to Lyn, that had to mean his entire relationship with Aaron was a lie. That would also mean that his mother was right about Aaron. He'd been so sure she was wrong, but apparently she was right.

He and Aaron were supposed to make it work long distance, eventually pick a place to live, and move in together. Lucky would be a famous artist; they'd have a gaggle of kids and be sublimely happy. Maybe three months wasn't long enough time to be together to have such fantasies, or take those fantasies seriously, but Lucky had had them, and now he was kicking himself for being so stupid. All the hiding, all the secrets, even Lyn with her "boy troubles." His hands clenched. Okay, he was heading for anger now, which meant that he was out of denial.

What the hell had Aaron being trying to do? What was the point of stringing him along all summer and making him think they had a future? Had he been nothing but a fling after all? He didn't understand any of it.

A throat cleared behind him, almost indiscernible over the sounds of the carnival behind them and the ocean waves crashing.

Lucky turned to see Aaron standing there, looking distraught. Anger bristled under the surface. A million things churned in his head and yet he couldn't find the words to say of them. He could only stare at Aaron and wonder why.

AARON DIDN'T HAVE TO GO far. Lucky was at the pier, sitting on a bench near where they'd kissed the other night. He didn't know what to say, only that he had to explain this whole mess somehow. He sat next to Lucky on the bench, contemplating his words.

"I can explain," he finally said.

Lucky didn't look at him.

"No, need," Lucky replied softly. "You're engaged to be married. That's pretty self-explanatory." He sounded hurt, and Aaron swallowed hard around the lump in his throat.

"You don't understand," Aaron told him. "You have no idea."

"I don't need to." Lucky glanced at him, and Aaron's heart sank at the expression on Lucky's face. His normally open expression had been replaced by one that was closed off. And Aaron had put it there. "You're engaged. Congratulations. I hope you and Lyn will be very happy together."

"Lucky, please just let me…" Aaron started to explain, but Lucky cut him off by holding up a hand.

"There's only one thing I really want to know." Lucky's voice was low and rough, as if he was trying not to cry. Bile rose in Aaron's throat; the urge to get sick was overwhelming. He swallowed hard, forcing his stomach to settle. "Obviously there was no point to whatever we were doing here. Why…" He paused, and Aaron's breath caught. "Why start something? Do you get off on stringing people along? What was I? Just something fun for the summer before you went back to your perfect life?"

"No!" Aaron shouted. He put his hand on Lucky's arm, but Lucky shifted away. Aaron let his hand fall into his lap; tears burned in the corners of his eyes. "You have no idea what this summer has meant to me." His voice cracked. "I love you, Lucky."

"Aaron, I just watched you propose to *someone else*. A *woman*. Forgive me if I don't quite believe your sentiment."

"Stop pretending you know anything about me or my life!"

Aaron had had enough. He couldn't take this, not from Lucky, not from someone who was supposed to love him unconditionally. Yeah, he'd screwed up. He should have told Lucky how things were from the beginning, and maybe this wouldn't have happened the way it did.

Maybe he wouldn't have hurt Lucky so much. Aaron wasn't the guy that Lucky thought he was and he needed Lucky to know that.

"You don't know anything about me!" Aaron shouted.

Lucky leveled him with a stare that was a punch in the gut. "Yes, I'm becoming very aware of that."

Aaron struggled for something to say, something that would convince Lucky, and himself, that he wasn't a horrible person and that they had something worth saving.

"If you were with Lyn, you should have just told me from the start," Lucky said quietly.

"I'm not!" Aaron said. "If you'd just let me explain—"

"Explain what, exactly?" Lucky shouted. He stood up and moved away from Aaron. Anger radiated from Lucky in waves, and Aaron trembled. He'd screwed this up so badly. "That you've been leading me on this whole summer, letting me think there might be a chance for more? Was I some kind of last hurrah? A way to get it out of your system before you settled down?"

"Lucky, no, I didn't! I don't want to marry Lyn!"

Lucky's eyes narrowed and his expression hardened. He was shutting Aaron out, he wasn't hearing him.

"Your proposal says otherwise," Lucky said, his voice flat.

"It's expected. It's been planned since Lyn and I were babies. Probably since we were in utero." The words spilled from his mouth. "My parents—you don't understand how they are. I can't tell them about me, or about us." He rushed through his words, nearly stumbling over them in his haste to get them out. "I can't be publicly gay, Lucky, I just can't. I'm going to take over the family business and—"

Lucky held up a hand to cut him off. Aaron wanted to move toward Lucky, to take Lucky in his arms. He wanted to beg and plead for Lucky to understand.

"This is what I know," Lucky said when Aaron stopped talking. "Either you're a liar or you're a coward. The fact is, I can no longer believe anything you say to me." The words hit home; an ache formed in Aaron's chest. He breathed in sharply. "Either way," Lucky continued, "I won't be your dirty secret any longer. I'm done."

"Lucky, please—" Lucky brushed past him without a word, headed toward the carnival lights. "Lucky!"

Aaron sank onto the bench, staring until Lucky's retreating form disappeared into the darkness. He couldn't feel anything; the weight of his family's expectations dragged him into an emotional abyss. He'd just lost the best thing that had ever happened to him and he had no one to blame but himself.

LUCKY MADE HIS WAY BACK to the trailer on autopilot, not taking in anything as he made his way through the darkness. It was done. He and Aaron were over. He let himself into the trailer and was glad to see it was empty. He had no idea where Bud and Walter were. Hell, he and Walter hadn't spent more than five minutes together the whole summer. Lucky sat on the edge of his bed. His hands shook, and tears welled up in his eyes. He sniffed them back, taking a deep, steadying breath. This would not break him. He was stronger than this.

He lay back on the bed, staring at the ceiling and trying not to think about last week, when Aaron had been in this very spot, posing naked so Lucky could draw him in the position he found the most erotic. *All of that couldn't have been a lie, right?*

He hated this; he couldn't stand it. He sat back up, staring at his things: his sketchbook, filled to the brim with drawings of Aaron; the shirt he was wearing the first time he and Aaron kissed; the shorts he'd been wearing the first time he and Aaron had sex; the receipt from their dinner date.

Lucky groaned. He couldn't even escape Aaron here. There was only one thing he could do.

He had to get out—away from the carnival, away from the beach, away from Aaron.

The decision seemed so simple once he thought of it. Lucky leapt up, grabbed his bag, and put it on the bed. He didn't bother with folding his clothes, just threw them in the bag. He was packing up the last of his art supplies when Bud walked in. Lucky didn't say anything, just continued to shove his things into his bag.

"Where's the fire?" Bud asked, and Lucky paused, glancing at him.

"What?"

Bud gestured to Lucky's frantic packing. "Someone die?"

"No." Lucky paused just long enough to make sure all of things were packed, that he hadn't left anything behind. He wished he could push all his emotions into a box and stow them away as easily as he could pack up his things.

"What's got your goat, then, son?"

Lucky tried to form the words, to tell Bud what had happened, but he took one look at the man and suddenly all he could see was Aaron in twenty years, married to Lyn. Lucky shook his head, choking back his tears. "I can't," he managed to get out. "I have to go."

He shoved open the door, nearly taking out Walter as he did so. Lucky headed across the trailer yard, headed for the boss's office.

"What crawled up his ass and died?" Walter asked behind him, but Lucky disappeared into the office before he could hear Bud's answer.

He had to get out of there. Tonight.

It wasn't until he reached the bus station that Lucky let the reality of the situation sink in. Once he'd fed the boss at the carnival a line about a family emergency—his heart was broken, wasn't that enough?—he'd headed straight to the station. Lucky's mind churned as he went through the motions of updating his ticket and finding a seat to wait for his bus.

He was angry; angry at Aaron for lying to him and leading him on, angry at Aaron's family for not letting Aaron be who he was, angry at Lyn, for being a friend while stabbing him in the back and ending up with Aaron as her husband. And he was angry that he was going to have to call his mother and tell her that once again, she'd been right. Lucky had been stupid—he'd fallen for the first guy to look his way, ignored all the warning signs that things weren't right, and it had blown up in his face. He finally understood why his mother refused to have a social life. It hurt too damn much when the people close to you inevitably let you down. If nothing else, Dinah Luckett knew that relationships ended.

Now Lucky knew it too.

Picking up the phone to call his mother was the hardest thing he'd ever had to do. Hearing her voice over the phone triggered another round of tears and they spilled over onto his cheeks as he explained to his mother what had happened. She didn't say she'd told him so. Instead she agreed to pick him up from the bus station on her way home from work.

As Lucky made his way onto the bus, he let out a shaky sigh. He wouldn't let himself be this foolish again. The bus pulled out into the night, and Lucky leaned his head against the cold glass, staring into the darkness.

Nothing this summer had turned out the way he'd hoped it would.

Chapter Seventeen

AARON WOKE UP LATE SATURDAY morning, exhausted. For a moment, he couldn't remember why he felt so awful. Then the memories returned, playing like an video he couldn't turn off. The events of the entire night plagued his thoughts and then his dreams, from proposing to Lyn to Lucky walking away from him. He had no idea how everything had gotten so screwed up. He'd fallen for the man of his dreams, but even that hadn't stopped him from proposing to Lyn.

His family had left him alone all morning; he'd made no move to get out of bed. Aaron assumed it was Lyn's doing. The guests had cleared out by the time he'd returned last night. Lyn had waited for him on the porch. He'd shaken his head at her, fighting back tears, and she'd given him a sad smile.

"If it helps at all," she'd whispered as they parted for bed, "it's a beautiful ring."

It hadn't helped, of course, though he appreciated that she tried. He couldn't bring himself to tell her he hadn't been the one to pick it out.

Aaron was no closer to any answers by the time he dragged himself out of bed and to the shower. He couldn't let things between him and Lucky end this way. He had to try again.

He got out of the house undetected and headed for the carnival. It was incredibly crowded. The holiday weekend at the end of summer had made people anxious for one last ride or plate of deep-fried carnival food. Lucky would be leaving for school next week, and there was a chance that Aaron would never see him again. He had to fix this somehow and he had to do it today.

He headed directly for Lucky's booth, intent on setting record straight even if he had to interrupt Lucky at work. When he reached the booth, his heart sank. Lucky was nowhere in sight. Aaron sighed. Aaron's texts and calls to Lucky went unanswered; he wasn't surprised, just disappointed. He was running out of options.

He turned away from the crowds and made his way toward the trailer area. If Lucky wasn't at work, then Aaron might find him there. At least there they'd have some privacy. He knocked on the door and was startled to see it opened by Bud, the roommate who'd walked in on him and Lucky. Aaron's face flamed red at the sight of him, but he ignored his embarrassment.

"He ain't here, son," Bud said.

"I'm sorry, I don't mean to put you out, but could I maybe wait for him?".

"He's gone, boy. Packed up and hit the road last night."

Aaron's legs nearly buckled. Lucky was gone; Lucky had left the carnival, possibly left the state, left *him*. He'd hurt Lucky so badly that Lucky had done what he could to get as far away from him as he could.

Aaron hadn't known he could hurt someone that much. He'd had no idea that he could hate himself this much either.

"You the one that made him up and go?"

Aaron nodded woodenly. Of course he was.

Bud gave him a long look and then stepped back into the trailer. Aaron figured he was going to shut the door in his face, and who could blame him, really, but he didn't. "You're letting in skeeters, boy. Get in."

Aaron blinked at Bud but forced himself to step into the trailer. The door shut behind him with a final-sounding click. He stopped, staring at Lucky's empty side of the room. Everything was gone. He tried to swallow the lump in his throat. Lucky really was *gone*.

Bud walked around and sat on his own bed. He stared at Aaron. "That boy loves you," he said.

"I know," Aaron whispered. "I screwed up. He was so hurt." He found himself sinking down on Lucky's bed, unable to remain standing. He tried not to think about the last time he was in this bed, about how he'd bared himself body and soul to Lucky, and about the love they had shared afterward.

He'd never have that again, and it was nothing less than what he deserved.

"What'd you do?" Bud asked.

Aaron couldn't believe that Bud wasn't throwing him out. Instead, he was asking Aaron to explain, to talk about it. He didn't know what to think; Bud was just sitting there looking at him, clearly waiting for him to start talking.

Aaron took a deep breath and the whole story spilled out, months of keeping everything silent leading him to divulge it all in a torrent of words: his parents' expectations, Lyn, his sexuality, and Lucky. He left out nothing; tears trailed down his face as he reached the end.

"Not the story you expected, I'm sure," Aaron mumbled, staring at his hands.

Bud chuckled. "You might be surprised."

* * *

The bus ride home gave Lucky time to think about things he didn't want to think about. He tried drawing, but every sketch turned into one of Aaron. He finally settled on listening to instrumental music on his phone and sleeping the trip away.

Getting off the bus was a relief. His mother met him at the bus station, took one look at him, and shook her head. She hugged him tightly, surprising him. Lucky couldn't remember the last time they'd hugged.

They didn't speak as he followed her to the car. He was grateful she didn't have an earful of lecturing for him. Instead, they spent the drive home discussing his school plans: when was he going to leave, what he was taking, and everything other than the reason he was home a week early.

He let her lead the conversation, content to follow along and not think about anything. His mother was the perfect distraction until he could leave for school, and he planned to use it to his full advantage.

He'd spent so long in the trailer that he'd forgotten what it was like to live in a slightly larger area. He'd forgotten what personal space was like, the knowledge that he could go to his room and shut out the entire world.

He needed distraction, so he shut himself away and tried to lose himself in his art. It worked for a bit until Lucky focused on what he was drawing.

Aaron's eyes stared up at him from the sketchpad. Lucky made a frustrated noise and threw it down onto his bed.

Even his art was failing him.

* * *

Aaron sighed as he approached the front patio of the beach house. He'd spent as much of the last few days as he could with Bud, reveling in the similarities of their situations. He had never considered that there were others like him, who would marry a woman because it was expected. The time he'd spent with Bud had been eye-opening.

He was sad to be leaving; he and Lyn had finished packing last night, and they would be driving away in a few hours.

He would be going off to school in a few days, and the best—and worst—summer of his life would be nothing but a distant memory.

Lyn was sitting on the porch, clearly waiting for him. He sat beside her.

"So he's really gone," she said.

Aaron nodded. She snuggled up next to him, leaning sideways in her chair, her arms slipping around his neck. Aaron tried to take comfort in her touch but, at the same time, he longed to feel Lucky's arms around him again.

"Any suggestions on what I should do next?" he asked her, desperate for some kind of guidance. Bud hadn't wanted to offer him any advice, feeling that he'd made the choices he'd made for his own reasons. He'd told Aaron that all he could do was trust himself.

Aaron didn't know where to begin.

"How far are you willing to go?" Lyn asked him with a questioning glance. He took in her red-rimmed eyes, her drawn expression, and the anger in her voice. There had been a lot of yelling the last few days, and it showed on her face. The parentals were furious at her refusal to marry Aaron.

"What do you mean?"

"I think it's time we take charge of our lives, Aaron," she said.

This wasn't the first time they'd talked about doing such a thing. It had been brought up idly over the years, but neither of them had taken the idea seriously. At least, Aaron hadn't. He wasn't sure about Lyn now, because she looked and sounded deadly serious. Maybe that's what she'd been doing all summer long. She'd been taking charge of her own life.

Aaron let out a bitter laugh. "Yeah, let me get right on that."

"You love him, right?" she asked. Aaron turned to look at her so fast his neck cracked.

"Yes, of course I do." It was the first time he'd admitted that to anyone but Lucky and Bud. It was such a freeing feeling, knowing that someone else knew.

"Enough to risk it all?"

"I don't understand, and it's not like that matters at this point." He sighed. "Lucky's gone; he's not answering my texts or phone calls. He wants nothing to do with me."

"Not if I have anything to say about it," Lyn said, standing up. He stared at her, his mouth falling open. "You're gonna fight for what you want and so am I."

"Lyn, what are you doing?"

"Aren't you tired of pretending, Aaron? I know I am." She cut him off. "Don't you want more from life than what our parents want for us? Don't we deserve to be happy?"

He hurried to follow her into the house, wondering what she could possibly be up to. He caught up to her, and she smiled slyly. "I have a plan."

They found their parents in the kitchen, enjoying glasses of sweet tea. They were invited to join them. He knew the parentals were hoping this meant that Lyn had finally caved, that she would be marrying Aaron as expected. Lyn hadn't told him what the plan was. Her only instruction had been to go with what she said, no matter what. He hoped he could do this. Freedom was dangling before his fingertips and he was so close to reaching out and grabbing it with both hands.

Lyn was a sight to behold as she stood in front of their parents. Aaron had no idea what she was planning, what she could possibly say to change the course of their lives, but he was game for it if she was. He was already living the worst that could happen. It could only get better.

"Aaron and I are not getting married," Lyn began, her voice firm but calm. "We're eighteen. We're adults. We have the right to make our own decisions." She glanced at him quickly. "While we love each other as friends, we're not going to marry each other because it's what you want. We're done being your puppets."

Their parents burst out into various exclamations, ranging from anger to shock.

"If you're finished," Lyn said, and their parents went quiet. Aaron was in awe. He'd never seen anyone take control of their parents this way. Why had it taken him and Lyn so long to get to this point? "Aaron's gay. It's not something he can change, and I don't want him to be stuck married to me, unhappy for the rest of his life. *I* don't want to be unhappy for the rest of my life. He's my best friend, and I'm not going to let anything get in the way of that."

The sounds that echoed through the room at that pronouncement made Aaron wince. The moment he'd dreaded for so long was finally here. At least they knew now.

"Aaron, what is she talking about?" Jennifer's voice rang out; his mother seemed near hysterics. He closed his eyes, inhaled and then exhaled slowly as he gathered his courage. Lucky had called him a coward and he had been, but not any longer. He was strong enough for this.

"I'm gay," Aaron repeated, opening his eyes to stare directly into his father's all-too-knowing gaze. He let his feelings about what had transpired at the party fuel him. He could do this.

"What is this rubbish? What are you trying to do, marrying my Evie to a–a degenerate?" Ronald shouted at Aaron's father. Charles said nothing, and Aaron knew then, in that moment, that he had lost his father for good.

"I'm not a degenerate!" Aaron surprised himself at the surety of his own voice. "I'm gay. Get over it." He almost clapped his hand over his mouth when he realized what he'd done, but he didn't. He'd never spoken to another adult, let alone Lyn's parents, so disrespectfully. Losing Lucky had triggered a release. Nothing mattered anymore, and he was so very tired of pretending it did.

"It's just a phase," Charles jumped into the conversation, his steely eyes washing over Aaron. Aaron held firm this time, not letting his father get to him. "You know how kids are these days."

"No, it's not," Aaron said. Lyn's mother let out a distressed sound. "I'm gay."

"And I'm not finished," Lyn snapped, directing the conversation back to her. He'd never seen Lyn snap their parents either.

"I'm in love with someone else and so is Aaron. We deserve to explore those relationships and see where they go—you, society, and the company be damned."

Susan, Lyn's mother, put her hand to her chest, as if her heart was breaking. Aaron's mother was crying into her handkerchief. The room was quiet except for his mother's sobs. Ronald looked angry. Aaron's father looked disappointed; Aaron glared at him until he turned away.

Until just days ago, Aaron would have been ashamed of his behavior, of his feelings of anger toward his father. Not any longer, though. Not after what his father had made him do in front of Lucky, had made Lucky witness. Aaron wasn't sure he could forgive his father for that. He and Lyn standing up for themselves and taking control of their lives was the least of what his father deserved.

"I'm in love with Richard Peterman," Lyn said into the silence. "He asked me out before school ended and swept me off my feet."

"Richard Peterman!" Aaron exclaimed, startled, snapping his head around to look at her. He stared at Lyn. Of all the names that could have come out of her mouth, that was not one he would have ever expected. On top of that, he felt stupid and guilty for not realizing she was going through the same situation he was: in love with someone she couldn't have. He hated that they'd drifted apart over the summer, but he wouldn't let it happen again.

"Yes," Lyn replied, blushing a little. "He's nothing like his father. He supports me, loves me, and wants me to have the things that I want."

"And what's that?" Charles asked, an edge to his voice.

"The company, of course."

The room exploded with noise again, all four parents yelling over top of each other. Aaron could see they weren't taking this well.

"I've enrolled at South University in the fall, for business administration. Aaron doesn't want the company." More enraged shouting filled the room, but Lyn pushed onward. "I want it."

Aaron felt that familiar queasiness for a moment, but then he pictured Lucky and that made him feel better. He could make it up to Lucky if he was free of all this.

"This is how it's going to be," Lyn finished, "Or we'll leave."

Aaron nodded in agreement, but he hoped it wouldn't come to that. He had no qualms about walking away now. Lyn would be with him. His trust fund had been given to him when he'd turned eighteen. There was nothing stopping them, except themselves.

"What will people think?" Jennifer cried. He resisted the urge to roll his eyes. Of course that was the first thing his mother would say; so much for any concern she might have about her son. No, in true Ledbetter fashion, she was more concerned with appearances.

"Which scandal do you think you could handle more? The one I'm suggesting or the one where we run off and have nothing to do with you? What would become of the company?" Lyn took Aaron by the hand. "We'll let you have some time to decide."

She led him out of the room, and Aaron likened his feelings to the way one would feel when being let out of jail.

"Oh my God," he gasped once they were outside as joy welled up inside him. He grabbed Lyn, picked her up, and swung her around. She shrieked and let out a happy laugh. "Why didn't we do this sooner?"

"You weren't ready." Lyn told him quietly, and he set her down on her feet. "I knew you would be one day, though, that you'd be brave enough, and we could both get what we wanted. Of course, if I'd had any idea how long it would take you…"

"Hey!" Aaron exclaimed in mock protest. "Thank you," he murmured, kissing her on the cheek. "Thank you for being the best friend I've ever had."

"Right back at ya," Lyn smiled.

"Now," Aaron said, giving her a grin, "what's all this about you and Richard Peterman, and why am I just finding out about it now?"

Chapter Eighteen

LUCKY LET HIS FIRST SEMESTER of college overwhelm him in all the best ways. He dove headfirst into his classes, and explored the material to its fullest. He was consumed by writing papers, he honed his art skills, and he only let himself think of Aaron in the dark of night before he fell asleep.

Leaving Georgia had been a coward's way out; after a few weeks at school Lucky was kicking himself for it. He'd just been so angry, his fight or flight response had kicked in, and he'd given in to the urge to flee without thinking about it. The few days he'd remained at home, he'd kept his phone off. He couldn't talk to Aaron, couldn't think about Aaron, and couldn't even put a pencil to paper without wanting to dissolve into tears.

That hadn't lasted long, with moving into school and getting settled. He'd had to turn his phone back on since he needed to use it for school. He'd managed to delete all of Aaron's texts and voicemails without reading or listening to them. His mother had suggested a clean break, that Lucky delete Aaron from his life.

Lucky wasn't sure it was working. Aaron might be gone from his phone, gone from his life, but he wasn't gone from his heart or his mind, and that showed nearly every time Lucky tried to create something.

When he had a set project, his art turned out the way he wanted. When he tried to draw or paint just because, his subject was always Aaron: Aaron on the beach, Aaron staring off into the sunset, Aaron on the pier, Aaron, Aaron, Aaron. He'd forgotten how to draw anything else.

It was Lyn who finally broke the stalemate of the situation. Staring at her number lighting up his caller ID, he very nearly didn't answer, but curiosity prompted him to take her call.

"Hello," he said into the phone.

"Lucky, hi," Lyn replied, sounding nervous. "I wasn't sure you'd answer."

"I almost didn't."

She sighed softly.

"I wouldn't have blamed you," Lyn said. "You have to know, I assumed he'd told you. And I had no idea about the party, or I would have never..."

"Lyn, what do you want?" Lucky tried not to snap at her. He had a project due on Monday and he needed to get started on it. Talking with Lyn and dredging up painful subjects he was doing his best to forget would not help him.

"I wanted to apologize, for one," she said. "You don't know how sorry I am. How sorry Aaron is."

Lucky flinched at Aaron's name. It was the first time he'd heard it since he'd left the beach.

"Sorry doesn't make it okay, Lyn," Lucky told her.

"I know," Lyn agreed. "Aaron said you blocked his number."

"I couldn't..."

"Yeah," she said, exhaling loudly. "Look," Lyn began after a quiet moment, "This is the only time I'm going to get in the middle of this. He doesn't know I'm calling and if he did, he'd probably kill me, but I thought you should know what happened after you left."

Lucky took a deep, shaky breath. If Lyn and Aaron were already married, he had no idea what he would do. Eighteen was surely too young to marry, and he'd assumed that they would have a long engagement. Didn't high society weddings take years to plan? But maybe they *had* gotten married already. Maybe their parents pushed them into an early wedding.

Watching them get engaged had been one of the worst moments of Lucky's life. Knowing that Aaron had gone through with the marriage might kill him, if one could die of heartbreak.

"Aaron and I stood up to our parents," Lyn said. "We told them we weren't getting married."

As it often did at the mention of Aaron, Lucky was pretty sure his heart skipped a beat. "That's… not what I was expecting you to say."

Lyn chuckled softly. "You should have seen our parents' faces. You'd have thought we'd just admitted to robbing banks or something." Lucky stayed silent and let her keep talking. "We told them that Aaron didn't want the company. He's not going to Harvard, either."

Lucky was at a loss. He must have made a noise of some kind because Lyn kept talking.

"He's trying to figure out what he wants to do with his life, now that he gets to choose," she said. "The only thing he knows for sure is that he loves you and wants you in his life."

"He said that?" Lucky asked before he could stop himself. His heart ached. He wanted Aaron to say that to him more than anything, but he wasn't sure if he could get past the lying and the half-truths and watching Aaron propose to someone else.

"Yes, repeatedly," Lyn assured him. "I just had to ask you, is there a chance you can forgive him?"

Lucky sucked in a deep breath. "I don't know, but I miss him."

She sniffled. "He misses you too. I miss who he was when he was with you. You have no idea what you did for him, Lucky. How much you changed him just by loving him."

Lyn fell silent again, and Lucky didn't know what else to say. He couldn't promise anything. He didn't know what he felt about any of this new information, and he couldn't bear it if Aaron hurt him again. He wasn't strong enough to go through this a second time.

"Just... think about it," Lyn urged. "Really think about it."

"I can do that," he said, as if he'd be doing anything else at this point, after her call. The possibilities had already begun to tumble around in his.

"I just needed to know that I did all I could to help make up for the hurt we caused you," Lyn murmured. "If nothing else, I needed to know you were okay."

"I'm okay," Lucky replied automatically. Okay was a bit of a stretch, he supposed, but he wasn't curled up in bed wishing he was dead. That was something, right?

"Good. If you think you can find it in your heart to forgive him... or even if you can't... just, let him know. That's all I ask." She sniffled again. "He's not taking this as well as you are."

Lucky didn't know what she meant by that but couldn't bring himself to ask for more details. It was hard enough to ignore the worry that sprang up at her words.

"I can do that, too," he promised.

"Thank you. Bye, Lucky."

"Bye." He hung up and lay on his bed, his mind racing.

He thought about the situation while working on his art project, while eating with his friends in the dining hall, hell, even while he was asleep.

After a week of thinking and trying to figure out what he was feeling, Lucky took out his phone. He entered a familiar number, then pressed several of the keys, generating a text message he'd never imagined he'd send.

He took a deep breath.

It was done.

Aaron's first act when they got home from the beach was to find his own place. He'd already received his inheritance from his parents when he'd turned eighteen, so it was just a matter of renting an apartment he liked—and his parents would have hated, thus endearing it to him even more—as well as furnishing it. It was in Savannah, but far from his parents' house.

He threw himself into the project, recruiting Lyn when she wasn't busy with school to get her opinion on everything. The thrill lasted him a few weeks, and then Aaron laid down one night, exhausted. He'd found himself unable to get up the next day. The uncertainty of his future had caught up with him, and he didn't know what to do about it. Everything that had been planned for him for the entirety of his life was gone. He could do whatever he wanted.

Aaron had no idea what that was, and that was utterly terrifying.

He spent a lot of time debating about attending college. He'd withdrawn from Harvard, much to his parents dismay. Lyn had urged him to consider continuing his education, even if he wasn't going to pursue business and brought him applications for other schools.

It didn't escape him that most of them were for schools in the Chicago area.

They didn't talk about Lucky, even though Lyn had tried. She'd insisted he'd feel better if he talked about Lucky. Aaron knew better. Nothing would make him feel better, so he did the only thing he could do, and avoided the topic all together.

In his weakest moments, he would find that website Lucky had showed him, with the erotic art and that portrait; he probably stared at it more than was healthy.

Aaron sighed again and bit his lip, then reach out for his laptop. He booted it up and then opened his search engine, typing before he could talk himself out of it. At the very least, he could get Lyn off his back about school if he told her he was researching his options. A listing of colleges in Chicago popped up in seconds. The list was long; the number of websites to check out was enormous. He was about to click on the top one when his phone beeped.

He whipped his head around to stare at his phone, which was lying next to him on the bed. The text tone was one he'd set exclusively for Lucky. Aaron's heart pounded, and he felt more alive than he had since that last day with Lucky. Aaron wouldn't be able to handle it if it was something awful, if Lucky… he couldn't even think it. He closed his eyes and took a deep breath, trying to focus. He'd never know if he didn't look at it, and not knowing was definitely worse.

Aaron picked up his phone with shaking fingers, fumbling through his lock screen three times and swearing before he managed to get it open. He hit the text button and his messages popped up. He breathed in deeply again and then hit the button for Lucky's thread.

He read the text with wide eyes, almost disbelieving. He let out a combination laugh-cry that very nearly turned into a sob, and would have, had he not swallowed hard against it.

A wise man once said "To err is human, to forgive, divine."

Aaron couldn't believe it. Lucky was willing to forgive him, or at least maybe talk about it. He wanted to pinch himself. He'd assumed their relationship was over; he had no idea how Lucky could even consider forgiving him.

I've thought of this moment continually since that night and now I don't know what to say.

He sat up, waiting on pins and needles for Lucky's reply. Joy was humming through his veins.

I do enjoy it when you're speechless.

Aaron choked out a laugh. He needed to hear Lucky's voice. With shaking fingers he pressed the call button and waited for Lucky to answer.

"Hi," Lucky said.

"Hi. I feel like I'm dreaming."

"I'd offer to pinch you but there's a distance issue," Lucky replied. Aaron let Lucky's voice wash over him, relishing it.

"I can't believe you'd even consider forgiving me," Aaron said quietly.

"I won't lie, Aaron, I was hurt and upset and I'm still not entirely sure I understand everything fully."

"I'm so sorry." Aaron's eyes welled up again. "I never meant for that to happen. I didn't know what to do."

"Neither of us reacted well," Lucky said, and Aaron felt his heart swell. "You were in an impossible situation, and I didn't take the time to understand that."

"I lied to you, I kept you a secret, I—"

"Aaron, stop," Lucky shushed him with a gentle voice. "You don't have to keep apologizing." He paused. "What we need to figure out is where we go from here. I need to know if I can trust you again."

"Lucky, I…"

"We have time," Lucky replied. "Let's just talk and see how it goes."

"I can do that."

"I have to go work on a project," Lucky said. "Call me tomorrow?"

"I will. I love you, Lucky."

"I love you, too."

They hung up, and Aaron fell back onto his bed, his whole body trembled. Lucky was willing to try to work things out. Aaron wiped his eyes and then rolled over, nearly landing on his laptop. The screen blurred back into life; his previous search stared him in the face. Aaron grinned and clicked the first button.

He had decisions to make.

Chapter Nineteen

AARON DRIFTED THROUGH THE FALL at odds with himself. He wanted nothing more than to rush to Lucky's side, but he couldn't. He had to take it slow with Lucky this time. They had to talk, really talk, and make sure this was what they wanted.

He had to be open and honest, something he was struggling with because he was so used to hiding what he was feeling. Aaron kept having to force himself to answer with what he was truly thinking and feeling, instead of what Lucky might want to hear.

His therapist had taught him that.

He hadn't wanted to try therapy at first, but Lyn and then Lucky had insisted he try it, just to see if it helped. It had, much to his surprise. It was nice to talk and not be judged for anything. It was a novelty to present a problem and get real advice on how to handle it.

It was wonderful what therapy had done for his confidence, for his self-esteem, and for his relationships. He and Lyn were getting along better than ever. She spent tons of time with Richard, of course, as well as with Richard's family, though Aaron didn't envy her there. He had no desire to be in a room with John Peterman any longer than he had to. She was also busy with classes, but they still hung out a few times a week.

The scandal over their failed engagement hadn't done nearly as much damage as his father had feared. In fact, stock in the company had risen. It just went to show that people really did like drama. Since his and Lyn's rebellion, Charles Ledbetter had taken Lyn under his wing. She was his protégé, his heir apparent. Aaron was happy for her, but it still stung. His father had cast him side and replaced him with Lyn. He would be lying if he said that didn't hurt. He made sure Lyn didn't know that though; he wanted her to enjoy herself, to be happy, to get everything she had secretly wanted.

Lyn's parents were still in shock. They barely acknowledged Aaron's existence, which was strange, considering their previous ubiquitous presence. With Richard Peterman now a permanent fixture in Lyn's life, the parentals had had no idea what to make of the entire situation. The Rossmans had seemed to accept Lyn's new life with grace; her father bragged to everyone about how well she was doing in school, how she was going to take over the business, and how she'd managed to land an wonderful young man in Richard Peterman despite "everything that had happened."

Aaron's relationship with Lucky flourished. They texted many times a day, about anything that came to mind. The big discussions were saved for the weekends, when they could Skype for hours and say things that couldn't be said through text. He hadn't told Lucky about applying for colleges in Chicago yet—he wanted to wait until they were back on track. He didn't want to make it seem as though he was rushing their relationship.

Aaron debated bringing up going to college in Chicago during their phone call the coming weekend. He hadn't heard back from any of the schools yet, but he was sure at least one of them would accept him for winter semester; he'd gotten into Harvard, after all. He wasn't any closer to figuring out what he wanted to do with his life, but college would help with that, right?

* * *

Lucky was leaving his art history class when someone called his name. "Mr. Luckett!"

He saw his professor from painting classing rushing up behind him.

"I'm sorry, Professor Jergens, were you calling me?"

"I was, Lucky, I was," Professor Jergens replied, clearly out of breath. "I'm glad I caught you."

"Sure, did you need something?"

"I'm putting together an exhibition for the end of the semester, and I was hoping you might be willing to show something."

Lucky's mouth fell open. "Are you serious?" Lucky couldn't believe it. He was a first quarter freshman; he was pretty sure most people were sophomores before they were asked to exhibit.

"You're very talented, Lucky. I would love to have one of your pieces," Professor Jergens said.

"Wow, thank you! I would love to show something, I just don't know what."

"Bring your portfolio by my office later this week, and we'll find something."

Lucky agreed and set a time to meet with him. He practically skipped back to his dorm room, he was so excited. He couldn't wait to call Aaron and tell him the good news. He should probably call his mother as well, though he hadn't told her about him and Aaron reconnecting, so he wasn't sure he wanted to talk to her yet.

He put that out of his mind and started mentally going through his portfolio, trying to pick a piece.

"How was your week?" Lucky asked as he sprawled out on his bed. Aaron's beautiful face was on his computer monitor.

"Fine," Aaron replied. "I had dinner with Lyn and Richard the other night. I was very much a third wheel, but Lyn wouldn't take no for an answer. She says I need to get out more."

"Do you?"

Aaron shrugged. "I'm trying to figure things out. I can do that at home better than I can if I'm out and about."

Lucky nodded, worrying a little. He wanted Aaron to feel better about himself, to know that it didn't matter that he had no goals now. Everyone went through this; Aaron was not the first. "How's therapy?"

"Good." Aaron perked up. "We worked hard this week. So I wanted to mention something but I'm not sure how you'll react."

"You can tell me anything, Aaron, even if I don't want to hear it." He meant that. They couldn't go back to the way things had been over the summer. Aaron had to know he could trust Lucky or there would be no saving their relationship.

"Okay." Aaron took a deep breath. "I applied for college."

"That's great! I'm so proud of you."

Aaron grinned.

"Which ones?"

"A few in the Chicago area," Aaron replied. Lucky nearly did a jig on his bed. He could hardly believe it. This was turning out to be the best week of his life.

"Seriously?" He couldn't keep the excitement out of his voice. "You're coming to Chicago."

"Well, I don't know if I've gotten in yet, but… yeah." Aaron smiled at him again and Lucky couldn't help but smile back.

Lucky laughed. "You got into Harvard; I'm pretty sure you can get in anywhere. But my news pales in comparison, now."

"You have news? Tell me."

"So one of my professors asked me to take part in an end-of-semester exhibition," Lucky told him.

"Lucky, oh my God, that's huge!"

"I know, I know," Lucky said. "It's a really big deal for a freshman to be asked."

"What are you going to show?"

"I don't know yet, my professor's going to help me decide."

"I'm so proud of you, Lucky. I wish I could kiss you right now."

“You’ll be here soon enough,” Lucky whispered. “Then you can kiss me all you want.” There was a charged pause, and then they changed the subject back to Aaron’s dinner with Lyn and Richard the other night, complete with Aaron doing impressions of them. Laughing loudly, Lucky couldn’t remember when he’d last been this happy.

Chapter Twenty

Lucky jiggled his leg nervously as Professor Jergens went through his portfolio. He wanted something to leap out and grab the professor's attention, something that would definitely need to be in the show. He didn't want the professor to regret asking him to be a part of the exhibition or worse, tell him that he was no longer in it.

Professor Jergens shut the portfolio without a word, and Lucky's stomach dropped to his feet.

"These are all good, Lucky," he said.

"I feel a 'but' coming," Lucky replied, biting his lip.

"Not exactly. A couple of them would work for the exhibition."

"Okay..." Lucky trailed off. He wasn't sure where Professor Jergens was going with this.

"Do you have anything else?" Professor Jergens asked.

Lucky blinked at him, his heart dropping into his stomach. This was it then. Nothing in there was good enough.

"I... just my sketchpad," Lucky mumbled. "It's not anything spectacular."

"Could I see it?"

Lucky dug his sketchpad out of his bag and handed it over. He wasn't sure what Professor Jergens was thinking he'd find. It was just unfinished drawings: some of the beach and the carnival, but most of them were of Aaron. "This." Professor Jergens had the sketchpad flipped open to the one of Aaron in his favorite pose, the one just like that painting, the one where Aaron was naked and hard. Lucky's cheeks went pink. He'd forgotten that was in there.

"Um," he said. "That's not really for... public consumption."

Professor Jergens ignored him, instead flipping through the rest of the sketchpad.

"You should show a series," he told Lucky.

"What?" Lucky was feeling like a yo-yo. "A series?"

"Yes," Professor Jergens replied. "You clearly favored this model. The drawings are well done, the emotions in them real and tangible."

"Thank you," Lucky said softly. "A series..."

"You up for it?"

"Absolutely," Lucky agreed, reaching out to shake the professor's hand. "Thank you so much."

Aaron made his way off the plane and breezed through baggage claim and into a rental car in what seemed like record time. He grinned, excitement coursing through his veins. Lucky's exhibition was in a few hours, and Aaron couldn't wait, not only because he was proud of Lucky and his accomplishment, but because he would finally be face to face with his boyfriend after months of phone calls and text messages. He would be able to take Lucky's hand, touch his arm, hold him close, and kiss him.

Aaron could barely focus on checking in at his hotel and getting changed, he was so impatient for time to pass. He wanted to see Lucky and he wanted to see him *now*.

The best part was, Lucky had no idea he was coming. They'd talked about trying to see each other when Lucky was on break from school, but there was no way that Aaron would miss Lucky's debut as an artist. Aaron rushed through a shower and heard his phone beep.

Aaron slipped into his slacks and then picked up his phone. It was a text from Lucky.

I'm freaking out.

Aaron shook his head, smiling. He couldn't wait until Lucky and he were face to face and he could tell Lucky how amazing he was in person.

It'll be great. Relax.

He put on his white dress shirt and buttoned it up; his phone buzzed again.

Easy for you to say.

Aaron chuckled, typed a reply, and then slipped on his tie. He grabbed his wallet and phone and left the room.

Breathe. It'll be okay.

LUCKY HAD TO STOP HIMSELF from pacing back and forth in front of the art gallery. He was freaking out. He wasn't sure he could have a conversation with anyone, and he had to get it together

Texting Aaron hadn't helped him as much as he'd hoped it would. Lucky had considered inviting him, but he hadn't been sure they were ready for that yet. He also wasn't sure how Aaron would feel about being the subject of his show pieces, but Professor Jergens had been right—they were his strongest ones. He was kicking himself now though, because Aaron's presence would definitely help him get through this without losing his mind and botching this incredible opportunity.

"Lucky!" Professor Jergens called his name. Lucky took a deep breath, forced a smile, and turned to meet his teacher. He let himself be steered inside to stand with the rest of the students whose work was being shown and wondered if they were all freaking out like he was. Probably not; they all appeared to be older. He was the only freshman.

He took another deep steadying breath. He could do this. Lucky had the talent, he just needed to believe in it. Before he could blink, the gallery staff announced that the doors were opening, and Lucky went to stand near his section of the exhibit. He wanted to be ready for questions and, he hoped, praise for his work. He stared at the sketches in awe of the sight of them in their professional frames. He pinched himself discreetly, not wanting anyone to know what he was doing, but needing to make sure one last time that he wasn't dreaming.

It hurt.

He smiled.

Several people passed through his section as the gallery filled up. A few of them stopped and asked Lucky about his drawings. The one of Aaron in *that* pose garnered the most attention, with one person even offering to buy it. Lucky was startled, but he refused.

He was never parting with that one.

"*True Love*, huh?" Aaron's voice was in his ear, and Lucky jumped. Aaron grinned at him. Lucky could only stare at him, eyes wide. Aaron was there, standing right in front him. A second later and Lucky was throwing himself into Aaron's arms, being held tightly. It had been months, but Aaron's arms around him still felt the same. He never wanted to leave Aaron's embrace.

Aaron pulled back after a second and nodded at the sketches. "So?"

"Uh, yeah," Lucky said, wiping his eyes quickly. The last thing he needed was a meltdown in public. "I couldn't name the series anything else." They were silent for a moment, and then Lucky finally asked, "What are you doing here?"

"I couldn't miss this, not your first real show, and since I'm apparently on display..."

Lucky grinned sheepishly. "My professor said these were my best work."

"I see," Aaron said, moving forward to study *that* sketch. It hung in the middle of the group and left almost nothing of Aaron to the imagination except his face, which was shadowed. "I feel like I should probably be more uncomfortable with my..." he trailed off, waving his hand up and down at the sketch, "on display, but oddly enough..."

"Oh?" Lucky asked. He had hoped Aaron wouldn't be upset, but Professor Jergens had been insistent and Lucky hadn't had the heart to bring it up in case Aaron said he didn't want that. It appeared to be a non-issue, since Aaron wasn't demanding he take the sketch down.

"Yeah," Aaron continued, glancing at Lucky. His eyes were dark and intense, and Lucky sucked in a deep breath. "It's kind of… hot."

A cough sounded behind them, and Lucky was sure his face was as red as Aaron's when Professor Jergens stepped near them.

"Professor Jergens!" Lucky exclaimed.

"Just wanted to see how things were going," he asked, glancing from Lucky to Aaron.

"Great!" Lucky replied. "Someone even wanted to buy one, but… well I can't bring myself to part with it." He gestured at the center sketch.

"Ah," Professor Jergens said. "Well, we all have the one piece."

Lucky nodded. "Oh, this is Aaron Ledbetter, my boyfriend. He's visiting from Georgia."

"Your model," Professor Jergens replied. "It's wonderful to meet such an inspiring muse, Aaron."

"Thank you, but it's really all Lucky's talent."

"An artist might be talented, but without inspiration, there would be no art." With that Professor Jergens clapped him on the shoulder and moved on to the next student. Aaron stared after him with his mouth open.

"He's got a point," Lucky said. Aaron blushed again, and Lucky wanted nothing more than to kiss him senseless. He glanced at his watch: another hour before he and Aaron could leave and start making up for lost time.

Aaron thought he might crawl out of his skin. The last hour of the gallery showing had been a new kind of torture. Every time he and Lucky touched, even just a simple brush of their hands, was like a firecracker in his soul, a flame that burned brightly and wouldn't die out. He wanted nothing more than to get Lucky out of there and back to his hotel room.

He was feeling a little crazy by the time Lucky was set free from Professor Jergens' clutches.

"Um," he started, his nerves nearly choking him. "We could—I have—we could go back to my hotel?" Aaron finally managed to ask.

Lucky smiled at him during his attempt at speaking, as if he found it adorable, but then his words seemed to sink in, and Lucky's eyes went wide and much darker, which Aaron hadn't thought possible. Aaron couldn't look away.

"Okay," Lucky replied softly. Aaron let out a breath he didn't know he'd been holding and led Lucky to his rental car. *How long would it take for them to feel comfortable around each other again?* He hated that he had driven this wedge between them, that his lies and half-truths had broken Lucky's trust in him. Still, Lucky was here with him despite it all, so Aaron had to keep hoping they would finally get it all worked out.

He hoped it was sooner rather than later. He thought he might die if he didn't at least get to kiss Lucky soon.

Aaron steered the rental car through the streets of Chicago, thankful that he had gotten a deluxe model with heated seats. As much as he loved his convertible, it probably wouldn't hold up well during Chicago winters. They were quiet; Aaron was unsure how or if he should break the silence. The radio played softly, a melody Aaron couldn't place, as they pulled up in front of the hotel. Aaron took a deep breath and nearly jumped when Lucky's hand covered his own. He turned his head and met Lucky's knowing gaze. Aaron gave a little chuckle. He was being ridiculous. They both were. This was *Lucky*. This was the same guy he'd been Skyping with for the last month, the same guy he'd met over the summer.

Aaron got out of the car and took Lucky by the hand, leading him into the hotel and quickly up the elevator to his room. He found himself walking faster and faster as they neared his room. There was an urgency in the air that was palpable now and it settled over both of them. Aaron found his room and hurriedly slipped the key in the slot. He turned around to speak to Lucky and every thought promptly flew out of his head.

Lucky was *right there,* a hairsbreadth away from him, his dark gaze burning into Aaron's soul.

He acted on instinct, words failing him. Aaron grabbed Lucky by the hand, jerked him forward, and kissed him for all he was worth.

All the waiting, all the worrying, every conversation they'd had over the last several weeks, it had all led up to this moment. Aaron was finally back where he belonged, in Lucky's arms. They stumbled into the room; their lips were still joined as the door slammed shut behind them.

"I STILL CAN'T BELIEVE YOU'RE here," Lucky murmured into Aaron's hair. Aaron chuckled.

"I couldn't miss this," Aaron replied.

Happiness spread through his whole body, from his head to his feet.

"I was kicking myself for not inviting you…" Lucky trailed off. "I thought maybe it was too soon." He smiled. "I was wrong."

"Yeah?" Aaron asked, his voice light.

"Yeah."

Lucky let himself bask in the afterglow, keeping Aaron nestled tightly against him. A thin sheet was all they wore. Aaron seemed to need to be covered up even though they'd had their hands all over each other just moments before. It was just one more thing about Aaron that Lucky loved.

"So there's something I wanted to talk to you about," Aaron began. Lucky shifted in the bed so he could better see Aaron's face. Aaron looked serious, and Lucky didn't want to think anything bad. They'd worked themselves all out and were better than ever. Surely Aaron wasn't about to ruin that somehow.

"Anything," Lucky promised. He needed to keep an open mind and not assume the worst.

Aaron picked up a couple of envelopes from the bedside table. They were business sized, and Lucky had no idea what could be in them, until he read the return addresses. Names of several Chicago colleges stared back at him from the envelopes, and Lucky sucked in a loud breath.

"Acceptance letters?" he asked, hope and excitement slipping in his voice. He knew that Aaron had applied, but not that he'd gotten in anywhere.

"I have no idea," Aaron said, biting his lip. "I haven't opened them."

"Why not?" Lucky had no idea why Aaron would wait to find out about something like that, something that would affect his entire future. Lucky would have ripped into them the moment he got them out of the mailbox.

"I was waiting until…," Aaron trailed off. "I thought… I thought we could do it together." His eyes met Lucky's, and Lucky nearly got lost in them; Aaron was waiting for an answer, though.

"Of course. Open away."

Aaron held up the first envelope but paused with his finger just barely under flap. "What if I don't get in?"

"That's ridiculous," Lucky assured him with a soft kiss on the lips. "Any school will be dying to get you."

"This is our future in my hands, you know?"

Lucky swallowed hard and nodded. Aaron closed his eyes and then ripped into the envelope. He pulled out the letter inside with shaking hands and jerked his hand so it unfolded enough for him to read it. He scanned the letter quickly.

"Well?" Lucky asked, impatient. Aaron glanced up, wide-eyed.

"I got in!" he suddenly shouted. Joy filled Lucky and he kissed Aaron hard.

"Open the other ones," Lucky urged as he pulled back a little. Aaron did, excited to see a few more acceptances.

"Looks like I have some decisions to make," Aaron said, setting them down. Lucky pulled Aaron back toward him, kissing him again.

"You'll figure it out. You get to decide. Not me, not your parents, not Lyn."

"Wow," Aaron said. "I do, don't I?"

"Yep. It will be the first of many decisions you make on your own." Aaron suddenly moved, pushing Lucky onto his back. Startled and incredibly turned on, Lucky made noise in this throat. Aaron grinned at him.

"What are you doing?" Lucky asked.

"Making a decision."

Lucky forgot everything else when Aaron kissed him senseless.

Chapter Twenty-One

Deciding where to go to school was much harder than Aaron dreamed it would be. He was a wreck the week following the exhibition. He had to decide where he was going to go and soon, as well as figure out where he was going to live. When he had been headed to Harvard, it was all planned out for him: where he'd live, what classes he would take, what fraternity he would join.

Now he was freaking out.

"You okay?" Lyn asked, dropping into the chair across from him at the kitchen table. Aaron glanced up at her. He hadn't known she was coming for a visit today. He'd given her a key when he'd moved in, and it was unspoken between them—she could come and go as she pleased. This was a home for her if she ever needed it, and she didn't knock before entering.

"You ever feel like if you make the wrong decision, your whole life would fall apart?" Aaron asked.

Lyn let out an indelicate laugh. "Every day," she said, twisting the ring on her finger. *Wait a second. Since when did she have a ring on her left third finger...?*

"Holy crap, Evelyn Rossman, is that what I think it is?"

Lyn grinned and waved her left hand around. "Yeah."

"You got engaged and didn't call me?"

"You were with Lucky! God knows you two needed to work out your issues and then *work out your issues*," Lyn said, wiggling her eyebrows in a suggestive manor. Aaron turned bright red at the implication. "I wasn't gonna get in the way of that. Besides, I wanted to tell you in person."

"So, details." Aaron pushed forward.

"He took me out on his family's yacht," Lyn began. "He hired a string quartet, and it was just the two of us and my favorite dinner, and then he got down one knee…"

"Wow," Aaron said. He looked at her, his beautiful friend, his best friend, and added, "That's wonderful, Lyn. I'm so glad you got the proposal you always wanted. Mine was… halfhearted, at best. You deserved more. Better. I'm so happy you finally got it."

Lyn's expression softened. She kissed him on the cheek.

"We've set the wedding date for this summer," she said. "We want to get married where we fell in love."

"Wait, you're getting married on Tybee Island?" Aaron asked, his eyes wide.

"Yes. On the pier, Fourth of July weekend." She paused for a moment. "You're gonna be my best guy, right?"

Aaron was startled for the third time since Lyn sat down.

She laughed at his expression of shock. "Who else would I want to stand up with me?"

"I just figured you'd go more traditional."

"Nope," Lyn said, grinning. "Richard is more than willing to go with what I want, and the parentals have stopped arguing with me about things since we told them we were doing what we wanted."

Aaron just sat there for a moment, taken aback. Things were really so much different now. Even the stack of acceptance letters in front of him hadn't driven that home.

"*Well?*" Lyn asked.

"Of course I will! Did you really think I'd say no?"

"I wasn't sure what you'd do, honestly," Lyn told him. "But you said yes, and now we can totally plan a fabulous wedding in which I will *not* be marrying you."

"Ah, music to my ears," Aaron teased.

"Hey!" Lyn said, taking mock offense. They burst into giggles and it was like old times between them. "What's all this?"

"Trying to pick a school."

"You're going to college?" Lyn raised her eyebrows.

Aaron nodded, biting his lip. "In Chicago."

The squeal she let out was so high pitched, Aaron was pretty sure only dogs could hear her.

"Okay," she began, taking the envelopes, "let's pick you a college."

* * *

THE EXHIBITION HAD DONE AMAZING things for Lucky. He'd sold a few of the sketches; not for much, of course, but it was a beginning, and a big boost for his confidence. Professor Jergens had put in a few words with a couple of other teachers, and they had agreed to allow Lucky to take classes usually closed to freshman, in the next semester.

He couldn't wait until the end of the semester—he would be going home to visit his mother and he was hoping Aaron might be willing to go with him. Lucky wasn't sure how they'd get on; he was worried about that. But he still wanted his mother to get to know Aaron and, he hoped, figure out that not all men were awful. He wanted her to see that even if bad things happened, it was possible to forgive and try again. He wondered sometimes if his father had ever tried to come back but his mother hadn't let him. Lucky didn't like to think about that though, because that meant she would have kept his father away from him his whole life.

When there was just a week left, he brought up the idea of Aaron coming to visit him in their weekly video chat.

"Would you consider coming to see me for Christmas?" Lucky asked, once they had caught each other up on how their weeks had gone.

Aaron looked startled but then smiled. "Christmas in Chicago could be cool," he said.

"Actually, it would be Christmas in Texas."

"You… want me to meet your mom?" Aaron sounded surprised.

Lucky smiled. "Yeah," he said. "I want her to get to know you. I'm planning on keeping you around for a while, so…"

Aaron's cheeks turned pink, and Lucky resisted the urge to sigh dreamily. He loved that Aaron still blushed like crazy around him. He found it completely endearing and he was pretty sure he always would.

"Wow," Aaron murmured.

"You don't have to if you don't want to," Lucky told him. "I just really wanted to see you."

Aaron groaned. "You don't play fair."

"Never claimed I would." Lucky grinned. "So you'll come?"

"I would love to."

The rest of their conversation was filled with travel plans.

When Lucky hung up, he had to call his mother and tell her about it. He sighed.

She wasn't going to like this.

Aaron rushed off the plane, completely overwhelmed by the size of the airport. His plane had been delayed by weather, and he hoped Lucky would still be waiting for him once he made it through security. He collected his bag and made his way through the airport, and then he stopped. Lucky was standing there with a bouquet of flowers. Aaron couldn't help the blush or the smile that crossed his face.

"Hi," he said.

"Hi," Lucky replied softly. "I figured that flowers would have to do since PDA was probably not the best thing to do…"

Aaron nodded, taking the flowers. He couldn't wait until he and Lucky were alone though. He'd missed kissing and touching his boyfriend.

The drive to back to Lucky's mom's apartment was filled with Lucky pointing out various landmarks and telling stories about places they passed, all while Christmas music played softly in the background. They finally pulled up in front of Lucky's building, and Lucky grabbed Aaron's bag out of the back of his truck while Aaron got out and looked around.

"I'm sure it's not quite what you're used to…" Lucky trailed off. Aaron turned to look at him, surprised.

"Lucky, I don't care where you live, as long as you have four walls, electricity, and heat," Aaron told him. The nervous look on Lucky's face melted away. Aaron couldn't believe that Lucky, super-confident Lucky, had been anxious that Aaron would be snobby about where Lucky lived.

Aaron took Lucky's outstretched hand. He was about to meet Lucky's mother and he was freaking out.

"Just… one, thing, before we go in," Lucky said, pausing outside the door to his apartment. Aaron raised his eyebrows. "My mom… she's not real happy I have a boyfriend and while she says she's fine with you being here, I can't swear she won't say something rude."

"Okay," Aaron said slowly. "But she's okay with you being gay?"

"She's fine with my sexuality; it's relationships that are complex."

"Well, I mean, my dad forced you to watch me propose to someone else, so anything has to be better than that, right?"

Lucky snorted. "We can only hope."

LUCKY TOOK A DEEP BREATH as he opened the door and ushered Aaron into the apartment. He hoped his mother would be on her best behavior, but it was hard to say with her. He'd warned Aaron; that was all he could do, really.

"Mama, we're home," Lucky called out. He waited for a reply but there was none forthcoming.

Lucky sighed, walking into the kitchen and over to the fridge. He found the note from his mother indicating she'd been called into work. Lucky went back out into the living room where Aaron was still standing, bag in hand and looking uncomfortable.

"Looks like my mom got called into work," Lucky told him, reaching out a hand for Aaron. Aaron took it, smiling in relief.

"What does she do?"

"She's a waitress at the diner around the corner," Lucky replied, leading Aaron down the short hall to his bedroom. Lucky took in Aaron's face as Aaron took in his room.

"Your room is *you*," Aaron said, looking around at all of the art hanging on the walls. "I love it."

Lucky shrugged. "Thanks," he said. "I think it looks a lot better now that you're in it."

Aaron turned and looked at him, his mouth fell open, and his cheeks pinked. Lucky grinned.

"You say stuff like that just to shock me and make me blush, don't you?" Aaron asked, looking at him with a raised eyebrow.

"You're just now figuring that out?" Lucky asked, in a teasing tone. Aaron chuckled.

"I suspected."

"Can't help it." Lucky put his arms around Aaron's waist and pulled him close. "You look so damned cute."

"Lucky," Aaron protested, whining a little in what Lucky assumed to be embarrassment.

"You know," Lucky drawled heavily, "we're alone…"

"I knew I loved you for more than your looks. Those are some keen observation skills you got there."

"Shut up and kiss me," Lucky said playfully.

"What about your mom?" Aaron asked as he nosed into Lucky's neck. Lucky shivered, want shooting through him.

"She'll be a few hours at least," Lucky murmured, dragging his mouth along Aaron's jaw. Aaron made a noise in this throat that Lucky found irresistible, and he couldn't hold back any longer. He tilted Aaron's face up and pressed his lips to Aaron's. He sighed into Aaron's mouth, losing himself in the feel of Aaron's lips against his.

He pulled Aaron down with him onto his bed and the outside world ceased to exist.

* * *

AARON DIDN'T THINK ABOUT RUNNING into Dinah Luckett when he went to the kitchen for a glass of water. He'd stopped to pull on a pair of shorts and a loose T-shirt, not willing to run around someone else's house without clothes on. He'd assumed that she would be in bed, given the late hour.

He hadn't expected Lucky's mother to be sitting in the living room with all the lights out except for those twinkling on the Christmas tree. She was drinking a glass of red wine when he stopped short in the hallway. Their gazes locked, and Aaron didn't know what to do. Part of him wanted to flee back into Lucky's room, shut the door, and keep her out. A more rational part of him—the part honed by years of etiquette—implored him to go into the living room, join her, and introduce himself regardless of his state of dress. If she was going to continue to disapprove of his relationship with Lucky, he'd rather keep it between the two of them; Lucky wouldn't need to know that, even after meeting Aaron, his mother didn't support them.

Forcing a smile, he moved slowly into the living room, holding out his hand for Lucky's mother to shake.

"Hi, Mrs. Luckett, I'm Aaron. Aaron Ledbetter."

Dinah Luckett's eyes raked over him, as if judging him, and Aaron had never felt more naked. How was it possible that a woman he'd never met seemed to see so much?

She finally took his hand and shook it lightly. She pulled her hand away quickly and sipped her wine again.

Aaron stood there awkwardly. He bit his lip and gathered his courage. He couldn't let things between them stand like this. Lucky would want them to get along.

"You don't like the thought of me dating Lucky much, do you?" Aaron asked, sitting across from her. Dinah's sharp gaze landed on him again, and Aaron held it with his own.

"I don't like my boy being distracted," Dinah finally said.

"Distracted?"

"He's got talent," Dinah said.

"I know he does. He's brilliant."

"He doesn't need you mucking it up."

"I would never," Aaron replied, a pang going through him.

"You already have," Dinah shot back, emotion in her voice for the first time since he'd said hello. "You broke him with your lies."

"He's not broken. And he forgave me for that."

She snorted. "You didn't see him when he got back here. Art is feelings," Dinah pointed out, and Aaron sucked in a breath. "He couldn't do anything, because he was hurting over you."

"That was a misunderstanding."

"They always are," Dinah said with a nod. She paused and then said, "You broke him down. He didn't think he had anything left."

"Is that what happened to you?" Aaron nearly clapped his hand over his mouth, he was so shocked those words had passed his lips. He'd been taught to respect his elders, and that had been possibly the rudest thing he'd ever said to an adult.

"You've got a pair on you." Dinah narrowed her eyes at him.

"If I didn't, Lucky wouldn't be interested," Aaron replied, the words again coming out before he could stop them. *Who was this and where the hell had the real Aaron gone?* Or was this the real Aaron, the one who was free from expectation? He wasn't sure.

Aaron's heart pounded. He hoped he hadn't gone too far, that Lucky's mother wouldn't suddenly toss him out on the street at three in the morning. Suddenly she barked out a laugh. Aaron stared at her as she chuckled.

"I can see why he likes you," Dinah told him when she stopped laughing.

"Love, Mama," Lucky's voice piped up from the hallway. Aaron and Dinah turned to see him standing there in just his boxers with his wild hair bouncing as he rubbed his eyes sleepily. Aaron's mouth went dry and he tried not to have a reaction; he didn't want that with Lucky's mother sitting across from him. "I love him."

Dinah sighed.

"He's not Dad," Lucky continued. "He's not gonna do what Dad did. You can't keep blaming every guy for Dad's mistakes."

"It's been a long night," Dinah said. "I'm off to bed."

Lucky sighed and nodded and kissed his mother on the cheek as she moved past him to go to her room. They were quiet until her door shut.

Aaron got up, heading into the kitchen for his much needed glass of water. He downed the glass as Lucky wrapped his arms around Aaron's waist, and rested his chin on Aaron's shoulder.

"Let's go back to bed," Lucky said. Aaron nodded, setting his glass in the sink. "Oh," Lucky continued as they shut his door. "I don't just like you for your balls."

Aaron nearly choked, coughing hard before barking out a laugh.

"I mean, they certainly help, but I love you for you."

Aaron couldn't help the giggle that escaped even as he was completely touched by Lucky's words. They tumbled into Lucky's bed, laughing softly.

Aaron wasn't sure that Dinah Luckett would ever like him, but it didn't matter.

Lucky loved him and that was enough.

That was *everything.*

Chapter Twenty-Two

FLYING HOME WITH LUCKY FOR spring break was harder on Aaron than flying home with Lucky for Christmas; they were going to Georgia this time, to spend the week with Aaron's family. He'd barely spoken to his parents since he'd left Georgia for Chicago, school, and Lucky. He had a weekly phone call with his mother, a daily phone call with Lyn, and almost no contact at all with his father.

His mother suggested he come home for spring break and that he should bring Lucky with him. Lucky hadn't hesitated, even though Aaron wouldn't have blamed him if Lucky had turned him down flat. After all, the last time Lucky had met his father, Lucky had been forced to watch Aaron propose to Lyn.

It was just one of many things that made Aaron nervous about the coming week. His parents would finally see that it wasn't just a phase, that he'd been willing to walk away from everything for this wonderful, amazing man. Aaron wanted them to get to know Lucky, to love him like family.

He wanted that. Being accepted by his family had been something he'd discussed many times with his therapist, and ultimately it was her support that gave him the courage to bring Lucky home with him.

They landed, made their way through the airport, and collected their bags. Aaron scanned the crowd and found the chauffer with his name on a sign waiting just outside the doors. He took Lucky by the hand and led him to the limo, introduced himself to the limo driver, and let him take their luggage.

"I think I'm underdressed for this," Lucky murmured as they slid into the back seat of the limo. The driver shut the door behind them. Aaron laughed lightly.

"This is my parents making a statement," Aaron told him.

"And what exactly are they saying?" Lucky put his arm around Aaron's shoulders.

"That they have money and possibly that they didn't want me to rent a car just to come from the airport since my car is still at the house in the garage."

Aaron didn't want to say anything else; nerves jumped in his stomach like grasshoppers. He needed a distraction. He leaned up and kissed Lucky. Lucky started in surprise, but then cupped his hands around Aaron's face, holding it gently in his hand. He didn't know if Lucky was as wound up as he was, but this would certainly take the edge off.

LUCKY HADN'T EXPECTED TO MAKE out the entire drive from the airport to Aaron's family home. Home was a loose term though; they stopped at the gate outside the property and had to be buzzed in. He used the time it took them to go up the winding drive to calm himself. Officially meeting Aaron's parents while dealing with *things* below the belt was not an ideal scenario.

When they pulled up in front of the house, Lucky's eyes widened. He'd been expecting something large, of course, since it was a gated property.

"And they say things are big in Texas," Lucky drawled, staring up at the house. Aaron let out a soft laugh with a slightly flirty expression on his face.

"Well," he said with a pointed glance at Lucky, "some things are."

Lucky's cheeks warmed.

"Hah!" Aaron crowed as the limo came to a stop in front of the steps that went up to the front porch. "It's about time you blushed."

Lucky just shook his head. Lucky let Aaron slip out first, following with a little hesitation.

A shriek echoed, and then Aaron was tackled by a whirling mass of blonde hair.

"You're here, you're here," Lyn repeated over and over with her arms and legs wrapped around Aaron. Aaron held her around the waist, keeping her from dropping. Lucky smiled at them; he enjoyed seeing Aaron so happy. Aaron had told him that he and Lyn had grown apart over the summer and had spent a lot of time getting their relationship back on track. Lucky couldn't help but feel that some of that was probably due to him and he never wanted to come between Aaron and Lyn.

"And you're here too!" Lucky barely had time to blink before Lyn was throwing herself at him, hugging him hard enough to possibly pop a few bones in his back. Lyn could have made a killing as a chiropractor if she hadn't been so in love with the shipping business. "This week is going to be the best week ever."

Aaron snorted, and Lyn poked him in the stomach. "You're such a Gloomy Gus, Aaron."

"I'm just realistic, "Aaron replied. "My parents, your parents…"

"They'll get used to seeing you two together," Lyn told him.

"I thought they asked us both?" Lucky asked, and glanced at Aaron.

"They did," Aaron said, biting his lip. He was nervous. "It's just… they've never seen me *be* with a guy before, you know?" He paused. "There's a big difference between *knowing* I'm gay and *seeing* that I'm gay."

Lucky nodded. He hadn't considered that point and it added to the things he was already nervous about: his skin color, his lack of funds, and the fact that he was the main reason Aaron had walked away from the family business and all of his familial responsibilities.

"Come on, grab your stuff," Lyn said, getting Lucky's attention. "You've got time for a shower or a nap before dinner."

"Where are the parentals?"

Lucky smirked at Aaron's term for his and Lyn's parents. He wondered if they were aware that was how Aaron and Lyn referred to them.

"Our mothers insisted on a spa day since we were having company," Lyn answered. Lucky slung his bag over his shoulder and followed Lyn and Aaron inside the gargantuan house. Their footsteps echoed in the large entry hall. "Our fathers are at the office, of course. We won't see them before six, as usual." Aaron nodded but anger burned in Lucky's gut. Aaron's parents hadn't seen him in months, had barely talked to him since he'd gone off to school, and neither of them were home to welcome them?

Lucky didn't say anything, though. He'd bring it up later when he had a moment alone with Aaron. Lyn was still chattering away, going on about school and Richard and who knew what else as they headed down what Lucky was sure was one of many hallways. He was going to have to use the GPS app on his phone just to get around without getting lost. Aaron slowed to a stop outside a closed door.

Lucky stopped too, watching as Aaron's cheeks turned pink.

"Your room?" he asked, finally adding something to the conversation. Aaron nodded.

"Your mom said she made the guest room ready," Lyn volunteered, looking between them uncertainly.

"Of course she did," Aaron muttered. "Never mind that we're fully grown adults or that you practically live at my apartment anyway."

"Aaron, it's fine," Lucky tried to placate him. It really wasn't an issue to get worked up about.

"No," Aaron said. "I want you in here with me. I want to sleep with you in my bed."

"Bow chicka bow bow," Lyn chimed in, almost as if on cue.

Aaron clapped his hand over his face in mortification. "That was not what I meant, Lyn!"

"It wasn't?" Lucky asked, conveying teasing disappointment.

"Oh, God, I can't take the two of you together."

Lyn cackled evilly and slapped Lucky a high five when Lucky held up his hand.

"Look," Lyn said, "force the bedroom issue or don't. Take a joint shower or nap or don't." She leaned over and kissed Aaron on the cheek and then Lucky. "I have to go study for my econ quiz that my bitch of a teacher is insisting we have when we get back on Monday." She headed down the hall. "I'll see you at dinner."

Lucky wondered for a half a second where exactly Lyn was planning to study since this wasn't her house, but that thought was gone the moment Aaron opened the door to his room. Lucky took a deep breath and followed Aaron inside.

AARON WASN'T SURE WHAT TO expect when he led Lucky into his old room. There wasn't much in it, since he'd moved out last fall and then to Chicago. He wasn't surprised that his parents weren't there to greet them; he hadn't expected them to be there. He wondered what Lucky thought about it, but it really wasn't worth discussing. His parents would do what they were going to do, as they had his whole life, and there was nothing he could do to change that.

"So?" Aaron asked Lucky, eyebrows raised. He wanted to know what Lucky thought of his room.

Lucky took in the powder blue walls and the simple décor, grinning when he saw a large framed poster of *Starry Night* near Aarons's bed. "It's very you."

Aaron narrowed his eyes playfully. "Is that a good thing or a bad thing?"

"Oh, it's a good thing."

"Really now?" Aaron returned with a lilt in his voice that was suggestive. Lucky moved closer, dropping his bag on the floor. Aaron set his on his desk just in time to get an armful of Lucky, who kissed him soundly.

"Someone will probably come get us for dinner soon," Aaron murmured between kisses.

"'Kay" Lucky mumbled against his mouth.

No parents appeared for dinner that night. He and Lucky foraged for leftovers when they finally roused from their post-sex nap, then spent the day wandering around the museum they'd gone to last summer, checking out the new exhibits. They came home to find dinner for two waiting. Lyn and Richard were at a charity event sponsored by her sorority, and he had no idea where his parents were.

In fact, Aaron's parents managed to be conspicuously absent almost all of his and Lucky's entire visit.

Lucky seemed as though he was more upset about that than Aaron was. Aaron was mostly happy; seeing his parents meant he'd have to deal with them, and he wasn't sure he was ready for that yet.

Aaron was quite shocked by the text he got from Lyn on Friday, the day before he and Lucky would fly back to Chicago, telling him that he and Lucky needed to hightail it back to the house because all the parents were there, and dinner would be served soon.

Aaron swore under his breath and grabbed Lucky away from a slightly over interested salesgirl at the souvenir shop they'd wandered into.

"My parents are at the house for dinner," Aaron said as he and Lucky hopped into his car and they sped off.

"Oh?" Lucky replied, his tone belying something Aaron couldn't identify.

"Yes." Aaron glanced at him out of the corner of his eye.

Lucky shrugged, and Aaron made a mental note to ask him about it later. He didn't want to start a discussion—or a fight, if it came to that—when they were finally going to see his parents. They rushed inside, heading for the dining room. Aaron halted in the doorway;

Lucky stopped behind him. Everyone had already been seated, and food was being served by one of the maids.

Aaron's stomach dropped and he swallowed hard. He should have suspected this. He should have seen this coming a mile away. This was just like his father, to do this to him, to them.

He took a deep breath, stepping into the dining room.

"Mother, Father," he said smoothly. "Forgive us, we were out and lost track of time."

LUCKY DIDN'T KNOW WHAT TO expect when Aaron strode into the dining room. The faces of Aaron's parents, of the couple he assumed were Lyn's parents, as well as Lyn and presumably Richard—totally that dude she'd been making out with at the carnival over the summer—all staring at them. Lucky could only follow Aaron to the two empty chairs. Immediately, one of the wait staff came over and started serving his plate.

"We could have waited, dear, if you wanted to change into something more… appropriate," Susan said. She was looking at Lucky. His first instinct was to feel self-conscious, but he fought it. So what if he was sitting at the table in a paint-splattered dress shirt, over a white undershirt, with shorts and beat-up canvas sneakers. Irritating them at this point was a perk.

"Nah, we're fine," Lucky replied, smiling widely. "Hazard of the job, you know." He gestured to his shirt.

Aaron cut into his chicken breast and took a delicate bite. Lucky tried not to ogle his boyfriend right there at the table, but he didn't care. He was *angry*. Aaron's parents had been the ones to suggest he and Aaron visit, then spent all week avoiding them, only to try to make them feel like crap for being late for dinner on their last night. He nearly growled out loud.

"I don't believe we've been introduced," Lucky said, glancing around the table. "Other than Lyn, of course." Aaron choked on his food, swallowed, and took a sip of water.

"I apologize," Aaron said once he found his voice. "Mother, Father, this is Lucky. Lucky, these are my parents, Charles and Jennifer Ledbetter. Lyn's parents, Ronald and Susan Rossman. And that's Richard Peterman, next to Lyn."

Lucky nodded, it was as he figured. "Pleasure," he forced out, sounding as if it was anything but. Lyn's mother looked slightly horrified, but he observed Aaron's father giving him a shrewd look.

"So, darling," Jennifer said. "How has your week been?"

"Fine, Mother. Thank you for having us."

"Yes," Lucky added. "Thank you. It's not every day I get to stay at a former slave plantation."

Awkward silence fell over the table, and Lucky could feel all the eyes on him.

"Am I wrong about that?" he asked, sipping his soda.

"No." Aaron's father was the one to answer. Everyone else was too busy staring at their plates. "The house does have that history."

Lucky nodded. Silence reigned again; the only sounds were the scraping of silverware on the plates.

"So, Lucky, are you working on anything right now?"

Lucky glanced at Lyn who wore a soft smile. She was trying to help, but Lucky didn't feel like playing along.

"A painting," Lucky answered.

"Oh? Can you tell us about it?" Aaron's mother asked. "I do love artwork."

Lucky debated about his reply but stuck with his plan of making this the most uncomfortable dinner for everyone else. "Well, it's a painting of a sketch I did last summer," he began, reaching out a hand and covering Aaron's on the table next to him. Lyn's mother dropped her fork, but Lucky didn't look at her. "It's of Aaron, of course."

"Really?" Lyn's voice belied her interest, almost like the cat that swallowed the canary. He figured she knew what he was trying to do.

"Yes," Lucky said. "He's my muse." Aaron blushed and looked at his plate. "The day he agreed to pose for me was one of the most amazing experiences of my life." Lucky let the innuendo drip from his words. Both mothers wore horrified expressions, as did Lyn's father. Lyn had her face buried in Richard's shoulder, her body shaking. He was pretty sure she was laughing. Aaron was staring at him with wide eyes.

"Now see here, young man." Charles was angry. Good. Lucky was looking forward to this conversation. It was about time someone set this man straight. "That is inappropriate and I will not stand for it in my house."

Lucky stood up and dropped his napkin on the tabletop. "No, what's inappropriate is the way you treat your son."

"Excuse me?" Charles practically had steam coming out of his ears. Lucky made a mental picture. He'd like to practice with red paint and the illusion of steam.

"Did I stutter?" Lucky replied, close to snapping.

"Lucky, don't," Aaron murmured.

"I can't just sit here and put up with this," Lucky told Aaron. "And you shouldn't have to either." He looked at Aaron's parents. "You treat your son like shit."

"That is enough!" Charles shouted.

"I could go on," Lucky said. "Because you do. You forced him to do what you wanted for years, to do what was 'expected,' to never have an original idea." He glared at them. "That could be considered child abuse."

"I will not have this in my house!" Aaron's stood up. "I want you gone."

"I bet you do. I bet you'd love nothing more than for me to disappear from Aaron's life."

"That can be arranged."

"Father!" Aaron exclaimed in horror.

Lucky just laughed. "It kills you that you can't control him anymore, doesn't it?"

"I think you boys have overstayed your welcome," Charles said after a long moment. "I have some business to attend to, if you'll excuse me." He nodded to Lyn's parents. "My apologies."

With that, he left the room. Aaron's face fell and Lucky sighed.

"Mother, I…" Aaron began. Aaron's mother didn't look at him, just rose from the table. The Rossmans rose behind her and the three of them left the table without a word.

"That was the best thing I have ever seen. All that was missing was the popcorn," Lyn crowed when they were out of earshot, her face lit up with joy. "It's about time someone handed them their asses, right dear?" She turned to Richard.

"Whatever you say, darling."

Lucky chuckled. It was clear who wore the pants in Lyn and Richard's relationship. Aaron got up, threw down his napkin, and left the room. Lucky sighed; his smile disappeared.

Just great.

Aaron was pissed. He was beyond angry. He just wasn't sure who he was more upset with, his parents or Lucky. All he'd wanted from this week was for Lucky to meet his family, for them to all get along. He want his family to accept his choices, to accept Lucky. Aaron wanted his family to accept him.

He was pretty sure now that would never happen.

Lucky entered the room, and Aaron took a deep breath. "You couldn't leave well enough alone, could you?" he snapped. He turned around to see Lucky just standing there, looking relaxed. It made him even angrier.

"I'm not going to apologize," Lucky replied, "if that's what you're after."

"Of course not," Aaron exclaimed. "The great and powerful Jonas Luckett is never wrong."

"That's not true and you know it."

Aaron let out a wet, angry laugh. "I don't know anything, isn't that the point you were trying to make?"

"Aaron, what is this really about?"

"Why did you have to antagonize them?" Aaron asked as a few tears slipped down his cheeks. "Huh?"

"They were treating us like crap," Lucky replied. "They were treating *you* like crap. What did you expect me to do?"

"I wanted them to like you!" Aaron cried, his shoulders shaking with the force of his emotions. "I wanted..."

"You wanted them to like *you.*" Aaron closed his eyes against the truth, and a second later Lucky's arms slipped around him and held him tight.

Aaron let out a sob, clinging tightly to Lucky. He felt as if he was slipping into a well of nothingness. His own parents didn't care about him. They didn't accept him and they probably never would.

"You'll always have me," Lucky murmured in his ear. "And Lyn."

And Lucky just held him while he cried.

Epilogue

Aaron loved the feel of the wind in his hair and the smell of the ocean in the air. He couldn't believe the difference a year could make. He glanced at the passenger's seat and smiling as he took in Lucky's hair blowing wildly in the breeze. He resisted the urge to tangle his fingers in the curly locks.

"Eyes on the road, lover boy," Lyn's voice rang out from the backseat. Aaron could feel his cheeks turning pink as Richard laughed behind him and Lucky gave him a knowing grin.

"Agreed," Lucky added. "While my stunning good looks are distracting, I would rather not wreck."

"Shut up, all of you," Aaron said, his face still burning.

"Awww, you're still so cute!" Lyn cooed, reaching up to ruffle his hair.

"I will make you walk!" Aaron said, slapping her hand away as Lucky laughed at them.

"Oh, that's great, Aaron," Lyn said. "Make the bride walk to her wedding rehearsal. That's just great." She dragged out the last word as much as she could. "And even if you did, Richard would carry me, right, darling?"

"Of course, dear," Richard agreed, kissing her lightly on the nose. Aaron still found it interesting, watching those two together. He'd never once imagined it while they were growing up, but Richard Peterman was perfect for her. He was supportive of everything Lyn wanted to do, from school to taking over the family business one day. Lyn was right about him being nothing like his father. Aaron was ashamed that he'd judged Richard so harshly based on his family.

This weekend would be interesting, that was for sure. It would be the first time Aaron would be out in society since the scandal had made waves last fall: since he'd refused to marry Lyn, since he'd left it to his parents to explain that he was gay and that Lyn would be taking over the company one day. It would be the first time that Lucky would be seen with him in a society setting, where people he'd spent years bending over backwards to impress would now be judging him, and possibly shun him, openly.

He'd also be seeing his family for the first time since the disastrous dinner over spring break. Since that night, he'd barely spoken to his mother, and he hadn't spoken to his father at all. Aaron had told his mother that if they couldn't accept him, he wasn't going to force them. He'd only called again to let her know that he and Lucky would be at the wedding, at Lyn's request. He would be standing up for her and Lucky would be his date.

It had to be burning his parents up inside that there was nothing they could do about that, but Lyn's wants had won out over most of the wedding planning decisions, mostly thanks to Richard's unwavering support.

THE NEXT MORNING DAWNED BRIGHT and early. Lucky rolled over, startled once again by the view out of the window of the beach house bedroom he was sharing with Aaron. It was the same house Aaron, Lyn, and their families had stayed in last year. He wouldn't lie to himself or Aaron. Walking inside the previous afternoon had brought back some rough memories. The night Aaron had proposed to Lyn had hung over all of them until Lyn had broken the ice, telling him and Aaron to go find Aaron's room and make themselves scarce until the rehearsal dinner.

Lucky hadn't thought twice, but grabbed a startled Aaron by the hand and led him up the stairs. Then there hadn't been any talking; instead Lucky had set about memorizing Aaron's body with his fingers and tongue, washing away the previous summer and replacing it with something new.

The rehearsal dinner had not gone as badly as Aaron had feared. Aaron had been extremely worried about the reaction they would face, but there had been none. No dirty looks, no snide comments, and they hadn't been ignored. Aaron was pretty sure that Lyn had declared that it be that way, and Lucky went along with it. Did it matter as long as it had gone well? Watching Aaron at the altar, standing next to Lyn as they practiced for the next day put all kinds of thoughts in Lucky's head.

It might be too soon for that now, but if he had his way, he and Aaron would be up there one day.

AARON WAS NERVOUS ABOUT THE wedding, but not nearly as nervous as Lyn. He was startled to the see the bride pacing back and forth in her robe in her ready room, ready to bite at her fingernails.

"I can't do this!" she exclaimed, pouncing on Aaron the moment he walked in.

"Whoa, whoa," he said, grabbing her by the arms, mostly to stop her pacing. She was making him dizzy. "Breathe and tell me what's going on."

"I can't do this, Aaron, it's too much!" Lyn said, sounding nearly hysterical. "What was I thinking? I can't get married."

"Lyn—"

"Get me out of here!" she said, a wild look in her eyes.

"Lyn, stop for just a second."

"No, there's no time, we have to go!" She moved toward the door, but Aaron held firm.

"Evelyn Rossman, stop it right now and talk to me." He'd never seen her like this and he didn't know what to make of it. "I thought you loved Richard."

"I do," Lyn replied, her voice coming out soft.

"Then what the hell is going on?"

"I just kept thinking about you," Lyn replied, wringing her hands together. "About how this was going to be us and how much I hated it and..."

"Thanks," Aaron replied drily, not really taking offense.

"You know what I mean, jerk." Lyn punched him lightly on the arm, breaking the tension. "I don't know, I just... The reality of actually being married to Richard hit me and I felt trapped all over again. I panicked."

Aaron was silent, his thoughts whirling. He knew that feeling so well.

"Listen, if you don't really love Richard, if you're not ready to be married, if you truly want to call this whole thing off, I will get you out of here right now." Aaron paused. "But if, as I suspect, you're just afraid, then I want you to remember that no matter what happens with you and Richard, you've always got me."

The words hung in the air, and Lyn's eyes were suspiciously wet. He couldn't remember the last time he'd seen her cry.

"So?" he asked.

Lyn sniffled and dabbed at her eyes. "You made me cry on my wedding day!"

"That's what I thought." Aaron grinned. "Now come on, let's get you into your dress. There's a groom out there waiting for you."

Much later that night Aaron found himself hand-in-hand with Lucky walking along the pier. There would have been some déjà vu, but the wedding decorations were still in place. The decorations danced in the light wind that blew around them, putting the spray of the ocean and the smell of the salt into the air. Aaron took a deep breath, thinking how much had truly changed in a year. He'd taken control of his own life. He'd fallen in love and found someone who had made him want to fight for himself. He remembered how he coped, and what he'd felt about himself a year ago, resigned to a life he didn't want with no way to get out of it.

And then he'd met Lucky. Lucky had turned his world upside down, making him feel things he'd never imagined possible.

"The wedding was beautiful, wasn't it?" Lucky asked as they walked.

"It was," Aaron agreed. Lyn had looked gorgeous, so full of joy and love as her father had walked her down the aisle. Richard had been in awe of her, as he should have been. Lyn's momentary panic aside, she was truly in love with Richard, and Aaron hoped they would be as happy as he was with Lucky.

"Do you think that'll be us one day?" Lucky asked quietly, his tone belying his nerves. Aaron stared at him, wide-eyed. He couldn't find words and was barely able to force air in and out of his lungs. Had Lucky just…

"Was that an attempt at a proposal?" Aaron finally managed to get out, arching an eyebrow at Lucky.

Lucky tugged Aaron close. Aaron took that moment to bury his head in Lucky's neck, inhaling him.

"If I propose, you'll know it," Lucky said in his ear. Aaron shivered at Lucky's breath just barely touching the sensitive skin there. "But the thought of it…"

"Me too," Aaron pulled back long enough to look Lucky in the eye. "I know exactly what you mean. It was all I could think about today."

"Glad to know it wasn't just me," Lucky murmured.

They stood like that for a long while, letting the ocean air wash over them. "How did it go with your parents?" Lucky asked after a while.

"Can we not talk about them?" Aaron replied. He didn't want to think about his father's indifference or his mother's tears. His mother's parting words of "It should've been you" as his parents had taken their seats at the wedding would haunt him for a long while. "Tell me what your mom said when you called her."

Lucky sighed, pressing his forehead to Aaron's. "She said no, of course."

"Tell me you talked her into it," Aaron said.

"I think I can get her to agree for like a week or something… maybe." Lucky told him. Aaron grinned. He might not have much of a relationship with his parents now, but his relationship with Dinah Luckett had taken some interesting turns over the last few months. She'd warmed up to him, especially since he supported Lucky with his art. He was trying to get her to fly to Chicago for a week to stay with them in their new apartment.

Aaron took one last look around.

"Will you miss it here?" Lucky asked. Aaron was pretty sure this was the last time he'd be coming to Tybee Island, at least for a good long while. For so long it had represented freedom for him, but now that he had Lucky, he didn't need it anymore. Freedom was Lucky. Freedom was loving him.

"Not a bit," Aaron replied, and he meant it. He leaned up to kiss Lucky softly on the lips. Fireworks erupted over their heads seconds later, celebrating the holiday as Lyn and Richard were pelted with birdseed on their way to the limo that would take them on their honeymoon.

Aaron barely noticed the commotion; he was so wrapped up in Lucky. His eyes opened and met Lucky's gaze, seeing the love that burned brightly in Lucky's eyes.

He was truly free.

Acknowledgments

Thank you to everyone who helped make this book a reality. To my Interlude Press family, thank you for making my dreams come true. To my family, your love and support is the reason why this book got written. I hope I make you proud. To my betas, you know who you are, this book is what it is because of you. I cannot thank you enough.

About the Author

KITTY STEPHENS' WRITING ASPIRATIONS DATE back to her childhood, when she and her brother made up stories about characters in their favorite books. She eventually started writing stories in online fan communities, and majored in English at Ohio State University. She lives in Ohio with her husband and son. *Set Me Free* is her first novel.

Get to know the author on Tumblr at @kittystephenswrites and on Twitter at @KittyStephensWr.

One **story**
can change **everything.**

@duet**books**

Twitter | Tumblr

For a reader's guide to Set Me Free and book club prompts,
please visit interludepress.com.

Not Your Sidekick by C.B. Lee

Welcome to Andover… where superpowers are common, but internships are complicated. Just ask high school nobody, Jessica Tran. Despite her heroic lineage, Jess is resigned to a life without superpowers and is merely looking to beef-up her college applications when she stumbles upon the perfect (paid!) internship—only it turns out to be for the town's most heinous supervillain. On the upside, she gets to work with her longtime secret crush, Abby, who Jess thinks may have a secret of her own.

ISBN (print) 978-1-945053-03-0 | (eBook) 978-1-945053-04-7

Lodestones by Naomi MacKenzie

On the eve of a new school year, several groups of college students cross paths as they seek out a secret end-of-summer lake party—including Robin and Charlie, two inseparable friends who discover of the course of the twenty-four hours that their relationship is something much deeper than simple friendship.

ISBN (print) 978-1-941530-37-5 | (eBook) 978-1-941530-51-1

Summer Love edited by Annie Harper

Summer Love is a collection of stories about young love—about finding the courage to be who you really are, follow your heart and live an authentic life. With stories about romantic, platonic and family love, *Summer Love* features gay, lesbian, bisexual, transgender, pansexual and queer/questioning characters, written by authors who represent a spectrum of experience, identity and backgrounds.

ISBN (print) 978-1-941530-36-8 | (eBook) 978-1-941530-44-3

www.ingramcontent.com/pod-product-compliance
Lightning Source LLC
LaVergne TN
LVHW090938080826
845145LV00003B/790

* 9 7 8 1 9 4 1 5 3 0 8 0 1 *